Yule Be Mine

PIPER RAYNE

This book is a work of fiction. Names, characters, places and incidents either are products of the author's imagination or are used fictitiously. Any resemblance to actual events or locales or persons, living or dead, is entirely coincidental.

© 2025 by Piper Rayne®

Piper Rayne® registered in U.S. Patent and Trademark Office.

All rights reserved, including the right to reproduce this book or portions thereof in any form whatsoever.

Cover Design and Illustrator: By Hang Le

1st Line Editor: Joy Editing

2nd Line Editor: My Brother's Editor

Proofreader: Olivia Winston

About Yule Be Mine

When workaholic best man Carter arrives in Mistletoe Falls for his best friends' Christmas wedding, a town-wide Santa Festival and a misplaced motel reservation leave him with one option—beg the woman he once rejected for a room at her bed-and-breakfast. Unfortunately, that woman also happens to be the bride's sister...and the maid of honor.

To make matters worse, the bride and groom are delayed, turning Ashley and Carter into last-minute wedding planners, forced into a truce neither of them wants. But late-night checklists, a blizzard of holiday activities, and a charming small town turn their snark into sparks.

When they get snowed in and every near-kiss feels dangerously close to something real, Carter realizes there's more to December than year-end deadlines

As their truce melts, one question remains—is this a holiday fling, or the start of forever?

Yule

BE

Mine

I shut my laptop and scan my desk for a third time, making sure I have everything. I've cleared my inbox and set my out-of-office automatic reply. There are two weeks until Christmas, and I'm off until the new year, but being head of IT means I'll be tethered to my phone if any problems arise.

A knock sounds on my office door. My boss, Ralph, stands in the doorway. One might think from his candy cane tie that he's a jolly, festive guy, until they catch his bushy eyebrows drawn into a crease at the bridge of his nose and the sour way his lips turn down.

"Heading out?" he asks, as if he doesn't notice my closed laptop, which I'm about to place in my bag.

"Yes. Gotta catch my flight." I walk to the hook on my wall and grab my wool coat.

Ralph's frown deepens as though I didn't clear the fact that I'm taking this afternoon off months ago. "Just checking in about the Warwick account. With you being out of the office for so long, is it in good hands?"

I slip my arms through my coat. "Darnel and Yvonne have

it under control. I've brought them up to speed, and I'll have my laptop with me to check in regularly. You'll barely know I'm not down the hall." My attempt at humor doesn't loosen the tension radiating from Ralph.

"I still don't understand why anyone needs to take so much time off just for a wedding," he grumbles.

I suck in a deep breath, wrap my scarf around my neck, and slip on my gloves. "That's the good thing about vacation time. One can use it however they want."

I'm not trying to be an asshole, and I sure as shit can't get fired, but this is about the tenth conversation I've had with Ralph on this topic. As if I need to explain how I want to use my vacation time.

Just to be sure I don't lose my job this holiday season, I soften my response once more. "I'm going early to help them get everything together before the big day. It's a destination wedding, and they haven't been able to prep in advance because of their schedules. Besides, they're my two best friends, and I want to spend some time with them."

He grunts, apparently still not understanding. I assume he doesn't have anyone close enough in his life that he'd be asked to do something like this because the man is a workaholic.

Doug, Steph, and I were inseparable throughout college. Freshman year, Doug and I roomed together, and Steph lived on the girls' floor below. After one late night studying in the common area, we all became quick friends. We did almost everything together. During college, Doug and Steph were just friends, but after we graduated, they both moved to Los Angeles. Their friendship turned into something more, and romance bloomed. When I first found out, it felt weird to be a third wheel around them, but in the years since, I came to see how much they meant to each other.

A tightness squeezes around my chest as I bring my bag

over my head to rest the strap on my shoulder. "Happy holidays, Ralph. I'll see you next year."

Once again, my half attempt at humor spurs no laughter, but he does make his usual grunting sound like a farewell as I leave my office.

Three minutes and an elevator ride later, I step out onto the busy Manhattan sidewalk. I weave in and out between the pedestrians bundled up to weather the cold, past the holiday-decorated storefronts.

New York doesn't hit the way it once did.

I remember my first Christmas in Manhattan after moving from Oregon. I was awestruck by the way the city transformed into a holiday paradise. Every store window displayed a Christmas theme, and every department store played Christmas carols. Holiday markets were set up every few blocks with niche, interesting shops. The tree at Rockefeller Center stood tall and proud, lights glistening in the cold, dark night. Everything felt so magical.

And it's all still there. There's not one inch of New York that isn't dressed in some holiday garb, but the glisten has worn off a bit. Everything feels a little more tarnished now.

It's not the city though. It's me.

Lately, my entire life feels... blah. I go to work, come home, relax, and go to bed. Rinse and repeat. The things that used to bring me pleasure—going out with my friends, climbing the corporate ladder at work, playing in my dart league—no longer does it for me.

The melancholy feeling crept in early in the year after Faith and I broke up. At first, I thought it was just a funk over the end of our relationship, which would have been the first time I'd ever felt that way about a break-up, but it was the only explanation.

Then the feeling persisted, and after a while, it became clear to me that it had nothing to do with Faith. Sure, I'd liked her, and we got along well, but I certainly wasn't heartbroken when we broke up. We didn't want the same things. Things like commitment and kids. So, we went our separate ways—end of story.

That discontented feeling of my life hasn't waned, despite my efforts to push it away. The fact is—something in my life needs to change.

Back in my apartment, I zip my suitcase closed, then check my watch to make sure I'm running on time. The car I ordered should arrive any minute now.

When Doug and Steph told me they were having their destination wedding in Vermont, I didn't get it. It's an interesting choice, but Steph's twin sister, Ashley, owns a bed-and-breakfast there. I guess when Steph visited her sister last year, she fell in love with the small town and insisted to Doug that they get married there.

Which is all fine and good, except Ashley and I didn't exactly part on the best of terms the last time I saw her. And that's putting it mildly.

Thank God I'm not staying at her bed-and-breakfast.

Most people hate the airport during the holiday season, but I get off on the buzz of all the travelers. Everyone is headed somewhere with excitement and anticipation on their faces. I can't help but wonder where every person who walks past me might be going.

As I wait in the ride-share area of the airport in Vermont, I make up stories in my head about the people waiting around me. What they might be here for. Whether they're returning home or here to visit someone.

By the time my ride pulls up at the curb, the end of my nose feels like the tip of an icicle, and my cheeks tingle from the cold air. The sixty-year-old man gets out of the car to help me with my bags, but I wave him off, placing my bag in the trunk myself.

He shuts his trunk and sticks out his hand. "I'm Rich."

"Carter." I shake his hand, and his smile deepens, forming more wrinkles around his eyes.

"Let's get in. It's freezing."

We both settle into the SUV, me blowing into my hands to warm them.

"You're headed to the Elderberry Motel in Mistletoe Falls?"

"I am."

He veers the SUV away from the curb. "Beautiful little town. Especially at Christmas. The missus is always asking me to take her there this time of year."

"They go all out for Christmas?"

"Son, it's the Christmas capital of Vermont."

My forehead wrinkles. That's one fact Steph didn't inform me about. Though why would she? I could have researched this place before coming, but I'm here because it's where my friends want to get married. Plus, it's not like her sister wants to share her town with me.

"Sounds like fun." I pull my water bottle out of my bag and guzzle half of it. Flying always dehydrates me, short trip or not.

Staring out the window, the scenery changes from city to evergreen forest. The street is covered with a light dust of snow. Whenever the wind blows through the trees, some of the snow on the branches falls to the ground. The mountains rise in the distance as we make our way closer.

We drive on a two-lane highway for a while, seeing only an odd house or gas station dotting the landscape as we grow closer to Mistletoe Falls.

I plan to check in at the motel before heading to Ashley's B&B to check with Doug and Steph about our morning itinerary. Last time I talked to Doug, he mentioned that they were behind because Steph had been on set so much these past few months.

They're both in the entertainment industry. Steph has been pursuing an acting career since we graduated from college, and she finally landed a recurring role on a popular television series a couple of years ago. Doug spends most of his time managing her career and those of a few other up-and-coming actors.

It's been something witnessing their dreams coming true, but I wish I didn't have the feeling that I'm being left behind. Not because of anything they've done, but because I feel like I'm missing out on *something*. I can't figure out what.

In many ways, my life has just happened *to* me. Lately, I've been questioning who I am and what I want. I made all the decisions I thought I was supposed to along the way. I went to college, earned my degree, completed an internship, and started working in my field right after graduation. All for what? To be what? Now, I'm... here. And I don't feel as fulfilled as I should after doing everything by the book.

I shake the self-analysis that's been my life the last year when I see the sign on the side of the road reading, "Welcome to Mistletoe Falls."

Rich wasn't kidding. Mistletoe Falls puts my small town, Climax Cove, to shame.

Every building on Main Street is lined with Christmas lights, highlighting the building's shape, its doors, and its windows. String lights in the shape of snowflakes hang from one side of the street to the other. Big bundles of mistletoe wrapped in red ribbon are placed in the middle of the lights, and every ornate streetlight is wrapped in greenery with big shiny balls that reflect the lights around them.

"Is this the set of a movie?" I mumble.

My family are huge Christmas movie watchers, and every year we make a list of movies to watch. I'll miss most of it this year since I'll be here, but my sister, Brynn, promised she wouldn't let anyone watch my favorites until I get home.

Rich laughs. "Now you see why the missus loves it so much."

We pass by the town hall, where a huge evergreen is decorated with lights and Christmas balls. They probably plucked that tree right off one of the nearby mountains.

Everything about this town is welcoming. It may not be New York City, but there's still a bustle of people moving from shop to shop, packages in hand. Kids trail behind their parents, sucking on the ends of candy canes.

"It feels almost fake."

Rich meets my eyes in the rearview mirror and chuckles. "Nope."

We drive for a few more minutes before Rich turns off the main road. The red-and-white sign in the distance reads Elderberry Motel. Rich pulls into the parking lot and parks alongside the small reception room.

"Thanks, Rich." I climb out of his car, and he meets me by the trunk.

"You're welcome. Enjoy your stay. Maybe I'll see you having hot chocolate in the gazebo when I bring the missus. She always loves all the festivities they plan."

I lift my suitcase out of the trunk, and he shuts it. "Sounds good, Rich."

"Happy holidays." He smiles and walks to the driver's side, getting in and shutting the door.

I leave him a tip on the app and slide my phone back into my jacket pocket. I head toward the door that leads into the reception area. Before I can reach for the door handle, it whips open, and I find Santa standing there.

Not the real Santa obviously, but someone dressed as Santa. Several people actually.

I take a step back as they file out the door, one after the other. Some short, some tall, some old, some young. Each one smiles and nods at me or says "Merry Christmas" as they pass.

I'm not sure how many exactly pass me by the time the doorway is empty, but it's *a lot*.

A plump woman with white hair pulled back into a low

bun, wearing wire-rimmed glasses, stands behind the counter, smiling at me. If she were dressed in a red dress and white apron, she'd be the perfect Mrs. Claus. "Good evening. How can I help you?"

I wheel my bag behind me and walk to the counter. "I'm checking in."

"Oh?" Her welcoming smile drops.

"Is there a problem?"

"What name was the reservation under?" She reaches for a pile of index cards.

"Russell. Carter Russell."

She nods and shuffles through the index cards, biting her bottom lip. This doesn't seem like a good sign. After she goes through the cards a second time, sighing with each card, she looks at me and cringes. Definitely not a good sign. "I'm afraid I don't see your reservation."

I stare at her for a beat, unsure what to say. "I know I made it."

"Maybe it got lost, or I wrote it down for the wrong dates. Whatever happened, I apologize, but I don't have it."

I'm not an angry guy who can't control his temper. No need to panic. I don't want to make this little old lady feel any worse. She looks on the verge of tears. "Not a big deal. I'd like to take a room then."

Her expression falls further, and her eyes do fill with wetness. "I don't have any vacancies." When I stare at her blankly, she adds, "It's the Santa Festival this week," as if that explains it.

I blow out a breath and push a hand through my hair. "Santa Festival?" I quickly wave my hand because it doesn't matter what the Santa Festival is. "Is there somewhere else in town that might have some vacancies?"

Her lips shake, and I fear that pretty soon her tears are going to fall down her rosy cheeks. "Very unlikely. Any rooms nearby are booked more than a year in advance when the festival is going on."

"Great." Shit. What am I going to do? "Have you heard of the Silver Bells B&B?"

"Of course. Ashley is such a sweet girl." Her smile shines back, so I don't have the heart to tell her that "sweet" and "Ashley" aren't two words I'd put together.

"Is there a cab company I could call to take me there? I know Ashley as well."

"You do?" The tears have dried up, and she's happy again. "Well, why didn't you stay there in the first place?"

"Long story." I'm not telling this woman that I'd fear Ashley might cut my balls off with a butcher knife in the middle of the night.

The woman reaches under the counter and pulls out her purse. "C'mon. I'll drive you there. I'm Ester by the way."

"Good to meet you, Ester. I'm Carter. I appreciate the offer of a ride, but should you leave this place unattended?"

She walks past me toward the door. "It's just a bunch of Santas."

I chuckle. Her attitude reminds me of Climax Cove. It's pretty much the opposite of running a business in Manhattan, where everything and everyone is filmed or watched by security from fifty angles.

"Really, I can just get a ride-share or a cab or something."

She swings the door open, and a burst of cold air assaults me. "There are no cabs or ride-shares in Mistletoe Falls." Ester laughs as if the idea that there would be is the funniest thing she's heard all day.

"But I just got dropped off by one." I follow her and close the door to the reception area.

She glances over her shoulder as she walks through the parking lot. "That's just because you were coming out of the city. You won't find one to use in town." Ester stops beside an older, cherry-red Ford truck with the name of the motel on the side. "Hop in." She gestures to the other side.

I do as she says, throwing my luggage in the bed of the truck.

The thought hits me when we're pulling out of the parking lot that I'm about to come face-to-face with Ashley again, and I have to ask her to put me up at her place. I doubt she'll see me as a Christmas gift. At least I'll have Doug to play my bodyguard and hopefully Steph to convince her sister to give me a room.

Chapter Three

ASHLEY

I exit The North Star Market and smile at the abundance of Christmas decorations up and down the town's streets as I always do. Dusk is approaching, so the lights glow and glisten in the crisp night air. If it were snowing, I'd feel as if I'm in the middle of a snow globe, just as I did the first snowfall after I moved to Mistletoe Falls.

I love all holidays, but Christmas especially. It's my favorite time of the year, which was a plus when I decided to move here. Our town might be small, but there's a reason we're such a big attraction in Vermont at Christmas time. We know how to do it right.

The sidewalk is bustling, since it's the middle of Santa Fest. No complaints from me, since I'm sold out from not only the Santas arriving in town, but the tourists who flock here to cheer them on.

I bump into an attractive man who's maybe a couple of years younger than me. We both mumble apologies and try to step around each other, but we turn in the same direction and our shoulders bump into one another again.

"Sorry." My cheeks heat in embarrassment.

He looks at me and smiles, then he stills, his head tilting and his finger pointing as if he knows me. I know what he's going to ask before the words leave his mouth. "Aren't you that girl from the *Shelter Bay* show?"

I smile at the man, though I'm sure it's more of a cringe.

Being an identical twin, this certainly isn't the first time I've been mistaken for my sister. But now that my sister is a rising star on the television show *Shelter Bay*, this exchange happens more and more often. She plays the role of Iris, the small-town shop owner and plucky best friend to one of the main characters, but she's told me in confidence that next season, she'll be a main character herself. They're setting up her character to be the love interest of her best friend's older brother. Meaning these little conversations will start happening all the time.

I don't mind them necessarily, and I'm so happy for my sister's success. But when you're a twin, especially an identical twin, it isn't easy to carve out a place for yourself and have the world see you as two separate people with different personalities. It seems the universe wants to press on that wound a little more now.

"No, that's not me." I grip the grocery bag tighter.

"It's you, I know it's you. My girlfriend watches that show every week."

I give him a wan smile. "It's my twin sister, not me."

He frowns. "You don't have to lie to me. I wasn't going to ask for a picture or anything." He pushes past me, his shoulder purposefully knocking into me this time. "It's not even that good of a show," he mumbles.

I inhale a big breath and continue to my truck, reminding myself that while I love the holidays, many people find them a stressful, difficult time. Perhaps that jerk is one of them. I hope my sister doesn't get attacked by cyber bullies from any of these exchanges.

I start my truck and turn up the volume on the radio as I pull out of my spot and head home. I only play the holiday station during this time of year, and one of my favorite songs, "Rockin' Around the Christmas Tree," is playing. I push that guy from my head and sing along in my off-tune voice until I pull past the sign at the end of the driveway that reads, "Silver Bells B&B."

My pride and joy. I bought the business almost three years ago as a thirtieth birthday gift to myself. I went to school for hospitality and, after a decade of working for other people, I decided to work for myself. I'd always imagined running my own bed-and-breakfast, and when I stumbled upon the listing for this place because the owner was retiring, it felt like kismet.

It took me a while to rehab it and decorate it the way I wanted. Now it's complete, and I'm living my dream job. So I can't explain why I feel something is lacking. Maybe because all of those side jobs, that to-do list, is all crossed off, and I'm overthinking my life.

If only I couldn't hear my sister's voice telling me that a man is what's missing in my life.

The thought of my sister makes me frown. She was supposed to arrive a couple of hours ago but never showed up. I tried calling her and her fiancé, Doug, but neither of them picked up. I never asked for her flight information, something I'm kicking myself for now. I'm sure her flight was delayed, but it's not like her to not let me know—at least with a text.

I grab my bag from the back seat of the truck and head to the house, kicking the snow off my boots before stepping inside. I don't bother removing my coat or hat on my way to the back of the house, where the kitchen is.

I'm not surprised to find Santa Claus sitting at the kitchen table.

"You're a little early for dinner, Nick."

It's not his real name. But it didn't take me long that first year of Santa Fest to figure out that the participants prefer to be called by whatever moniker they adopt.

Presently, I have Nick, Nicholas, Kris, Mr. Kringle, and Mr. Claus staying with me. At least they're all different this year. Last year, I had three Nicks. When one of them would ask for something to be passed down at the dinner table, no one knew which Nick was asking.

He chuckles. An honest full-bellied Santa chuckle. Which spurs my laughter.

"I'm hiding from Mr. Kringle. He's such a blowhard. He keeps going on and on about how he's got the reindeer race in the bag." Nick shakes his head.

"Has he ever won previously?" I ask, setting my bag on the other end of the table and taking out the baking supplies for the pie contest, as well as some items for tonight's dinner.

"Not once. He usually comes in last."

A small laugh escapes me. I can't take sides when they're both my guests, so I change the subject. "Well, I'm making us a hearty stew for dinner, and I made some fresh bread earlier today. If you want, I can bring your dinner up to your room rather than you eating in the dining room with him."

He waves me off. "I'll be fine by dinner. I just needed a minute to myself." He pushes the chair back and stands. "Anything I can help you with?" Nick inspects the groceries splayed over the table.

"I appreciate it every time you ask, Nick, but you're my guest, remember?" I chuckle and bring the carrots over to the sink to wash and peel them.

"It's gotta be a lot of work to take care of everyone. I don't mind helping."

I glance over my shoulder and smile. Nick has grandpa energy, and he's stayed with me every year since I took over Silver Bells, so I have a bit of a soft spot for him.

"It's what I love doing though, so it doesn't feel so much

like work. You relax, and don't let Mr. Kringle get under your skin. Just show him who's boss at that race." I wink.

Nick sets his hands on his protruding belly and laughs. "Fair enough. Think maybe I should work on my Christmas spirit?"

"You have more than enough. We all reach our limit sometimes."

Giving him advice makes Carter Russell's face float into my head. Ugh. My sister's best friend is arriving today, according to the last time I talked with her. His presence shouldn't matter to me. We're not sworn enemies or anything, but our last interaction couldn't have ended worse, and truth be told, I'm a little embarrassed by my reaction. It might have been a little over the top, but my emotions got the best of me.

Ever since my sister told me she wanted her wedding to be held at Silver Bells and Carter would be standing up in it, I've vowed to keep my tongue-lashing toward him in check for the sake of my sister. I won't ruin my sister's wedding, and hopefully, Carter will agree.

"If you change your mind and need help with anything, let me know," Nick says, leaving.

I swing the door of the fridge open and grab the stewing roast. "Shoot." It seems like I have more immediate problems than Carter.

Chapter Four

CARTER

Ester pulls down the driveway for Silver Bells B&B, and I begrudgingly admit the place is charming.

The house is big and white with black shutters and a wraparound porch. Each column on the porch is wrapped in greenery with red ribbon woven through. The double door entry has oversized holly wreaths on each door, and warm light filters into the dark night from every window. The scene could be captured on a Christmas card.

The only part I hate about this time of year is how early the sun sets. By seven o'clock, it feels like midnight because it's been dark for hours.

How do people who live near the Arctic Circle deal with almost total darkness all the time through the winter?

"Here we are!" Ester turns the vehicle off and reaches for the door handle.

"Oh, no need to get out." I open the passenger door. I have no idea how this first meeting with Ashley will go, so we don't need anyone witnessing it.

She waves me off. "I might as well say a quick hello to Ashley since I'm here."

I give her a tight smile.

Ashley.

I'm not sure if it's because of the wedding, but she's been on my mind a lot lately. More specifically, the night it all went down between us. I've probably rehashed the whole scenario a thousand times over in my head. I could've handled things differently, better for sure.

This little reunion of ours in less than five minutes is bound to be awkward.

After I grab my bags, Ester and I walk toward the front porch. She doesn't bother to knock, just swings the front door open and strolls right in.

I follow, my gut churning now that I'm in Ashley's space. The house has a cozy vibe. There's a large living area to my right where a fire burns in the hearth, then a dining room beyond that with a long table. To my left is a library and another sitting room. The entire house exudes holiday warmth and charm from the garland along the hearth and doorframes to the gorgeous, flocked Christmas tree in the corner by the window.

"This time of day, she's probably in the kitchen preparing dinner. Come on." Ester marches toward the back of the house, and I wheel my luggage through, following like a well-behaved toddler.

As we grow closer to the kitchen, Ashley's voice rings out. "That's it right there."

A male grunt sounds, and I stop in my tracks, my luggage banging into my thighs from the abrupt stop.

"Just a little bit to the left," Ashley says.

Another grunt from the male.

"Perfect, that's perfect!"

Ester stops to turn and look at me. "Why did you stop?"

"Are you sure we should..." I point ahead of us toward the hallway.

It sounds as though Ashley's doing more than preparing dinner. I ignore the way my stomach feels leaden from the thought of her in there with someone else.

Ester's gray eyebrows crinkle before she shakes her head and continues forward. I guess I'm the only one who heard Ashley's instructions to her grunting male companion. She disappears around the corner, and when she doesn't cry out in dismay, I figure it must be safe to follow.

Following, I'm thankful to not find Ashley half naked on the counter, with a pants-less male grinding into her over and over. Instead, it's her and an older man half-dressed like Santa Claus trying to move the fridge back into place.

"What happened?" Ester asks.

Ashley turns and looks at us. Her eyes light up when she sees Ester, but when she notices me right behind her, her smile falls. She doesn't even give me a nod of acknowledgment. "My fridge crapped out. We pulled it out of its spot to see if we could figure out the problem."

"Do you even know how to fix it?" The words are out of my mouth before I have time to consider how Ashley will receive them.

She whips her head toward me and narrows her eyes. There's the Ashley I'm familiar with. "I figured if it was leaking something out the back, that would be a pretty obvious sign of what was wrong."

I raise both hands in a placating gesture that doesn't lighten the anger brimming in her eyes.

"One more push and that should do it," she says to Santa.

Santa's eyes widen, and the redness and sweat along his face say he's at about max capacity for physical exertion.

"Wait, wait. Let me help you." I step forward, unwilling to sit by and watch this old guy and Ashley struggle to move the fridge back into place.

"We don't need your help, Carter." Ashley's tone is sharp as a blade.

Santa heaves a breath and gives Ashley an apologetic expression. "Actually... I might have tweaked something in my back. Do you mind taking over for me? I'm gonna go have a hot shower."

"Of course. I appreciate your help." She puts her hand on his arm. "Let me know if you want a heating pad or anything later, okay?"

Santa nods and heads out of the room.

I put my hands on the fridge and press my body to the metal. "All right, on three. One, two—"

She shoves on two because... of course she does.

We wiggle the fridge back into place. Ashley blankly looks at me and mumbles a reluctant thank you.

"Did you figure out what happened?" I undo the buttons on my jacket.

"I don't know." Aggravation lines her tense body. She doesn't strike me as someone who handles not being able to figure something out herself well. "I pulled the roast out for dinner and noticed it was barely even cold in there." She opens the door and sticks her hand inside as if to demonstrate.

"I'll send my son over tomorrow to take a look," Ester says. "He's handy. Fixed one of our washers last month and saved me from buying a new one."

Ashley blinks in surprise. "How did I not know you had a son?"

"He lives a few towns over, which is why you haven't met him. He's helped me plenty around our place, and he'll do the same for you." Ester beams like a proud mother.

"Are you sure he wouldn't mind?"

"Of course not. He'll be thanking me for sending him after one look at you." Ester laughs while Ashley's cheeks grow pink. "He's single, and you two would be an adorable couple." Ester's eyelashes flutter.

Ester can leave now.

Shit, where did that thought come from? Ashley and I are nothing, less than nothing, we don't even like one another.

Ester's not wrong though. Ashley might look identical to one of my best friends, but I can objectively say she's not just attractive, but hot. Her long red hair hangs in waves to her mid-back, and her hazel eyes have flecks of gold near the center that catch in the light. Her curves only add to her appeal, and I remember back in college, more than a few guys appreciated her sister's matching ones.

"I appreciate it, Ester. Thank you."

"Don't mention it. So, how do you two know each other?" Ester waves her finger between us, looking curious.

Ashley and I glance at each other, both waiting for the other one to answer. Will the other tell the details of six months ago?

Unable to stay silent, I answer, "Ashley's twin sister is a good friend of mine from college, as is her fiancé." I keep my voice light.

Ester nods because it's believable. It's the truth, after all. I'm just leaving out that I know what it feels like to have Ashley's lips on mine.

"What are you doing here?" Ashley's eyes narrow, as though she's just now realizing that there's no reason for me to be standing in front of her, certainly not with the owner of the motel, and not with my suitcase in tow.

Ester sucks in a breath and cringes at Ashley's aggressive tone. "There's been a bit of a mishap. I misplaced Carter's reservation, so I don't have a room for him."

Ashley's head whips in my direction with wide eyes.

God, I hate being put at her mercy.

"I don't have any extra rooms either."

My stomach sinks. The thought of sleeping on one of those red park benches along Main Street washes through my mind. "Don't worry about me. I'll figure it out with Doug. That's why I'm here early."

Ashley's perfectly arched eyebrows furrow. "Doug and Steph aren't here yet."

"What do you mean they're not here? They were supposed to arrive before me."

She throws her hands up. "I don't know, Carter. I called Steph, and she didn't answer her phone. Neither did Doug. Maybe their flight was delayed, and they're in the air. Your guess is as good as mine."

"Oh no..." Ester wrings her hands.

The tension and annoyance in Ashley's face fall at Ester's worried look. It's a softer side that I've never seen from her before. "Don't worry about it, Ester. We'll get it sorted, won't we, Carter?" She steps over to Ester and squeezes her shoulder.

"Of course. It's no big deal." I give Ester a reassuring smile, and her head volleys between us before she ultimately nods.

"Okay, but if there's anything I can do, you let me know, okay?" Ester hems and haws as if she's unsure if she should leave.

Does she see it? The awkwardness we're trying to mask?

Ashley and I both agree that we will, and Ester hesitantly, almost reluctantly, walks out of the room.

"I could always share your bed?" I grin at her.

She gives me an expression like *I'd rather share a bed with The Grinch.* "In your dreams." I open my mouth to respond, but she beats me to it. "Oh, wait, that would be your nightmare, right?"

I sigh, shoving my hands in my jacket pockets. Neither of us has forgotten then.

Chapter Five

I can't believe I just told Carter that my ego is still bruised from what happened between us. Now he's giving me that look. The same one from that night. As if he's resigned to talk about it. Something I didn't want to do then, and something I still have no interest in doing now.

"I have to go grab some coolers to put the fridge stuff in." I weave around him, but he holds my wrist and brings me to a stop. Tingles race up my arm, and I hate my body for betraying me. We can't still want this man.

"We need to talk, Ashley." I meet his gaze, and our eyes hold for an uncomfortable beat.

He's as gorgeous as he was six months ago. Vibrant blue eyes set off by his dark-brown hair, broad shoulders, chiseled jaw, and just the right amount of five o'clock shadow to be sexy.

"I really need to go to the store, Carter. I have to prepare dinner for my guests." I give him a pleading look, asking him to drop this topic at least for the time being.

He nods and steps back. As I walk past him, his hand

wraps around my wrist again. "After dinner then. I don't want our… issues to cause problems at Doug and Steph's wedding."

"Isn't the problem what didn't happen?" I grab my purse off the kitchen table, snag my coat off the rack, and head out the door.

Carter's rejection should not sting after all these months, but it does, and I have no idea why.

That's a lie. I know exactly why. I thought we had connected that night. I thought he was feeling what I was…

I shake my head and start the truck. My cheeks heat in embarrassment.

At the hardware store, I grab a few coolers to store the food from the fridge in until it's fixed. Fifteen minutes later, I'm barely out of the truck before Carter waltzes out of the front door of the B&B.

"Figured I could give you a hand, so you can avoid a few extra trips in this cold."

"Were you stalking me out the front window or something?" I say rather than thanking him.

He doesn't say anything snarky back. He ignores my jab, takes two of the coolers, and walks toward the house. I follow with the third, silently reprimanding myself for making this so much worse. The immediate warmth of the house thaws my chilled bones. This winter has been brutal.

"This is a really great place," Carter says, watching me slip off my boots.

I walk past him and mutter, "Thanks."

Despite my saltiness toward Carter, I soak in the charm of what I've created as I walk through the hallway. Twinkling lights wind through garlands on the banister, casting a warm glow over the polished wood. Plaid ribbons, tiny ceramic villages, and bowls of ornaments are tucked into every corner. A towering tree I cut down myself glows in the front room, dressed in vintage ornaments and red-and-green-beaded garland. Faint Christmas music from my own specially made playlist drifts from the speakers, and the scent of cinnamon lingers through the air, thanks to bundles of sticks I've tucked into nooks and crannies. It's like walking through a living Christmas card. And I'm glad Carter appreciates my hard work, although I hate myself for needing someone else's praise.

Once we're in the kitchen, he continues helping me, the two of us wordlessly emptying the contents of the fridge into the coolers like our own two-man assembly line.

I'm so busy trying to preserve the food that it takes me until I'm passing him the eggs before I realize this isn't his job. "You don't have to help me."

He dramatically looks around the empty kitchen. "I don't see anyone else."

I stop handing him the egg carton and tug it closer to me. "I have it handled."

His head tilts, and he sighs. "Seriously, Ashley?"

We stare at each other as if we're in a standoff. I look into the cooler and realize I need to get this done so that I can prepare dinner. My to-do list is growing the longer I stand here, holding the carton as if we're fighting over the "It" toy on Christmas Eve.

"Thanks."

His smile is wide with victory, and I want to take it back. But Nick and the other Santas come to mind. This isn't about Carter and me, it's about my business.

"Just tell me what you need me to do." He releases his grip on the carton first. One small win at least.

"I have a chest freezer in the laundry room where everything from the freezer can go."

"Why don't you show me where it is, and I'll take care of that so you can get started making dinner for your guests?"

How does he expect me to stay irritated with him when he's making it so difficult? I show him where the freezer is, and he works on moving everything over while I try to figure out dinner now that stew is no longer an option. The stew meat in the fridge might be okay, but I'm not taking my chances on anyone getting sick and the health department coming knocking.

I decide to go with chili instead. I had planned that for tomorrow night, so thankfully, the frozen beef is now thawing and only partially frozen. After I put the meat in a pot to start cooking, I grab the green peppers and onions to chop.

Usually, I don't offer dinner for my guests, but during my first year hosting the Santas for Santa Fest, a bunch of them complained about how long it took to get into the restaurants in our small downtown. There's such an influx of people this time of year that our restaurants aren't equipped to handle the increased demand. So, I made it an option to add dinner, which makes me more money, and they don't have to worry about where to eat every night. It's a win-win.

Carter doesn't return to the kitchen. Pretty soon we have to talk about that night six months ago, and he probably doesn't want to do it while I'm holding a chef's knife. Can't say I blame him.

By the time the chili is almost ready, he still hasn't reappeared, but since I figure I should at least offer him dinner for helping me, I go to find him. I wasn't lying when I said I didn't have an extra room for him tonight, but I can't exactly kick him out either, so I'm not sure what I'm going to do. He won't be staying in my room, though, that's for sure.

Before I reach the great room to ask if anyone's seen him, I slip my phone from my back pocket and check again to see if Steph has texted me.

Nothing.

I fire off another quick text, asking if everything is okay and telling her to call me right away.

As I'm about to turn the corner, a roar of laughter rings

out over George Michael singing "Last Christmas." I peek around the corner to find Carter standing in front of the fireplace, telling the Santas a story about an ice sculpting competition he participated in with his family last Christmas.

I clear my throat, and the laughter dies, everyone turning in my direction. "Dinner's ready. Carter, you're welcome to join us."

The Santas head around me toward the dining room, Carter following.

"Appreciate it. Have you heard from Doug or Steph yet?" The concern in his voice makes me feel more anxious.

"Nothing yet. You?"

He shakes his head. "No."

"I'm sure we'll hear something soon." I give him a reassuring smile, trying to hide the fact that I'm worried too.

We've just sat down at the dining room table when my phone rings. Relief loosens the tension in my shoulders when I see my sister's name on the screen.

Standing from the table, I step out of the room to take the call. "Steph... hey. Where are you? Are you okay?"

"I'm fine. I'm so sorry I didn't call sooner." I assume she's at the airport from the sounds and voices in the background.

"That's all right. Did your flight get delayed or something?"

"Is that your sister?" Carter says behind me. Very, very close to me. So close, I smell his crisp cologne.

"Is that Carter?" my sister asks, sounding surprised.

"Yeah."

"Oh, good. That saves Doug a call. Doug?" she says into the phone without moving it away from her mouth. "Any chance you guys have time to FaceTime?"

Unease creeps into my stomach. Something is definitely wrong. "Sure... just give me a few minutes, then I'll call you."

"Great." She hangs up without even a goodbye.

I meet Carter's gaze. "They want to FaceTime with us."

His head tilts as it always does when he doesn't understand something. "Why?"

"I don't know. C'mon, let's go take the call in my office."

When we reach my office, I grab the phone stand I use if I'm watching something, so I don't have to hold it. I pat the seat next to me on the love seat and place the stand on the coffee table, facing us. I dial Steph's number, and she answers on the first ring.

My small office is the only place in the house that is just mine—besides my bedroom—so I sometimes like to read in here. The love seat always worked fine, since squeezing a full-sized couch in here would make it feel crowded, but now I'm wishing I could fit a sectional. Carter's thigh is basically pressed up against mine. How am I supposed to concentrate on my sister?

My sister and Doug's faces come on the screen, and they are not at an airport. Not unless Vancouver or Vermont planted a bunch of evergreens in the middle of their terminals.

"Steph, what's going on?"

"I'm so sorry I didn't call earlier. I was stuck on set, and I made Doug promise not to call either of you until I knew for sure what's going on."

"What *is* going on?" I ask at the same time as Carter says, "I take it you didn't make your flight?"

Steph cringes, and Doug wraps his arm around her shoulders in what seems like support. "No, and there's a bit of a problem."

I inhale a deep breath, my patience gone after the day I've had. "Oh my god, Steph, what?"

My sister fiddles with the end of her hair, always a dead giveaway that she's about to deliver bad news. "I'm stuck on set for another week."

"What?" Carter and I say at the same time.

"We have to do reshoots. They want to change some of the scenes and the script has undergone an overhaul…"

"Do I need to remind you that you're supposed to be getting married in ten days?" I toss up my hands.

Carter's hand reaches toward my knee, but when I glance at him, his hand drops back to his thigh.

"There will still be a wedding," Doug says, and I'm not sure if he's trying to convince himself or us.

"But there's so much still for you to do. How are you going to pull off a wedding in a few days?"

Steph and Doug look at one another, with smiles so suspicious that Carter and I glance at each other. "Well… that's where we were hoping you two could help…" My sister bats her big hazel eyes.

"What do you need from us?" Carter asks.

"The chairs need to be picked up," Doug says.

"And then have the bows put around them," Steph finishes.

I raise my hand. "Wait. I thought the event planner was taking care of that?"

Steph waves off my question. "I fired her. She didn't get my vision."

My mouth falls open. "You *fired* her? When?"

"We just weren't seeing eye to eye." She's so calm. Her wedding is in ten days, and she's not going to be here to plan it, and she acts as if she just left a week-long spa retreat.

"Well, maybe you should hire her back, Steph, since you won't get here until right before the wedding."

"Ash, I know you can do it. Mistletoe is your town. And you're the most organized, capable person I know. I should have asked you to be my wedding planner from the start, really. Plus, we're twins. We practically share a brain. You know what I like."

Once upon a time, that was true, but since the success of

Shelter Bay, she's changed. Not in a bad way, just different. Now, she tends to look down her nose at things she used to think were great. If I'm honest, I'm surprised she wanted to get married at my B&B. An overpriced venue in Lake Como is more her style.

"Please. Please, will you help us?" Steph puts her hand in a prayer pose and gives me her helpless expression that I fall for every time.

I'm going to help her. She's my twin sister, for heaven's sake. But I am slightly annoyed with her over it. Any sibling would be. "Of course I'll help."

"*We'll* help," Carter corrects.

I roll my eyes. "Yes, *we'll* help."

"Thank you so much!" The way my sister's face transforms with a big smile evaporates my annoyance.

"We appreciate it, you guys," Doug says.

"I'll email you everything unfinished on the list. And if you have any questions at all, call me. If I'm not on set, I'll be able to pick up. Otherwise, leave a message."

I sigh. I'm already busy enough through to this weekend because of Santa Fest. This is the last thing I needed added to my list. "Okay, as soon as you send it over, I'll take a look and let you know if I have any questions."

"You guys are the best! Thank you," Steph says, then someone calls her name in the background. "I'm needed on set again. Talk to you both soon."

She hangs up before Carter and I can say anything else.

"Unbelievable." I shake my head and grab my phone off the holder, standing.

"On the bright side, you have an available room, right?" Carter smiles. "Steph and Doug's room?"

Oh shit, he's right. "Yeah, it's right next to mine."

Chapter Six

CARTER

Although Ashley isn't excited about me staying at her B&B, she doesn't kick me out.

Part of me knew she wouldn't. She may not like me, but she's a good person, and no way she would send me out into the cold. Had it not been for Steph and Doug being unable to show up, I'm not sure if I could have convinced Ashley to let me sleep on the couch, though.

Walking into the room that would have been theirs, I'm sure it's the nicest room in the place. It's got its own bathroom, a wood-burning fireplace, a small seating area, and even a window seat that overlooks the spacious backyard and the line of evergreen trees beyond. It even has its own fully decorated Christmas tree tucked in the corner.

Getting to stay in this room is the only good part about my two best friends being unable to get here to plan their wedding. The worst part is that I have to work with Ashley to set everything up. Not because I don't like her, but because she doesn't like me. Then again, maybe it's a blessing in disguise. Perhaps the two of us being forced to hang out together will help to bridge the distance between us. One can only hope.

The next morning, I join the Santas at the breakfast table at nine. Even though I met them all last night, I can't keep straight who wants to be referred to as Nick, Nicholas, or Mr. Claus. With so many variations, there must be duplicates. So instead of saying hello by their name, I go the generic route. "Good morning, gentlemen. What's on the schedule for today?"

"Candy cane eating contest," the one who I think refers to himself as Nick says.

"Interesting." I reach for a plate of bacon in the center of the table. "How does one go about devouring a candy cane? Are we talking chewing or sucking?"

The Santas laugh, and it's a big ego rush for me. They might be the happiest people I've ever met, or they are just really polite, since they laugh at everything I say.

Ashley breezes into the room, holding a plate of pancakes. "How about you stop corrupting my guests?" There's a lightness in her tone that wasn't there yesterday. Day two, and we're already making progress.

"Now where would be the fun in that?" I grin when she sits in the empty seat directly across from me.

She shakes her head, but one corner of her mouth turns up, as though she finds me amusing but doesn't want to admit it.

Something about her looks different today. I can't quite place it until I've finished loading my plate with the spread she's set out. Her hair hangs in waves down past her shoulders. She's curled it, rather than wearing it straight the way Steph does, and the way she wore it on the first night we met. She's also wearing a hunter green sweater—a color that Steph complained about one St. Patrick's Day when she showed up in red for us to go bar hopping, stating the color green only made her hair look more red. Seeing Ashley now, I can see Steph's complaint was justified, but in my opinion, it only makes Ashley look more beautiful. Her freckles are a little more pronounced and the gold flecks in her hazel eyes sparkle. Suddenly, my mind wanders to her under me as I thrust into her. In my mind, her red hair is wild, and her skin is flushed pink.

"Why are you staring at me?"

It's like a needle screeches across a record, stopping all fantasies, and I shake my head. Ashley's forehead is wrinkled as she glares at me. I guess we aren't playing nice anymore.

"Sorry, I was thinking...about something," I mumble, staring at my plate, forking some of the hashbrowns, feeling my cheeks heat.

What the hell am I thinking? Ashley is not hot. She cannot be hot. I've already been down this road. She's identical to my best friend. Looks completely the same as my other best friend's soon-to-be wife.

During breakfast, Ashley remains quiet. I'm not sure if it's because I'm here or if it's her usual demeanor, although I don't think so. As soon as breakfast is finished, all the Santas depart the dining room to get suited up for the day.

"Steph emailed her list overnight. When I'm done cleaning up breakfast, let's go over it." Ashley stands from the table, collects a few of the plates, and disappears into the kitchen.

I push away from the table, grab the other plates, and follow her.

Ashley sets the dishes on the counter beside the sink and turns, but she stops when she sees me. "What are you doing?"

"Helping you clean up."

"You don't have to do that." She takes the plates from me, her fingers brushing mine in the exchange. I ignore that same tug I felt earlier when she sat down at the table.

"I want to help. Many hands make light work, or whatever that saying is."

She looks over her shoulder, seeming like she's sizing me up. "Okay, thanks. I appreciate it."

Is it possible that Ashley has set down her sword where I'm concerned? I sure hope so, because it will make this next week more bearable.

"Do you mind finishing clearing the table while I rinse the plates and put them in the dishwasher?"

"Sure." I make quick work of clearing the table, having to ask a few times where things like the salt, butter, and syrup go. "Do you have a dishcloth I can use to wipe the table off?"

"Yup." She turns away from the dishwasher and walks to a drawer on the other side of the kitchen. "Right here."

While she's grabbing the dishcloth, I glance at the dishwasher. "You know you're loading that thing wrong, don't you?"

"There's not a right or wrong way to load the dishwasher." She tosses the dishcloth at me.

"There is, and you're doing it the wrong way."

Ashley huffs out a rush of air and crosses her arms.

"I'm only trying to help." I raise both hands. "Forget I said anything."

She leans against the counter, and her eyes bore into mine as if she wishes a giant pointy candy cane would strike me on top of the head. "Oh no, please... educate me, oh wise one."

I debate letting it drop, then decide otherwise. Motioning to the dishwasher with my hand, I say, "All the cutlery is faced down. They should be face up. It will be easier for the dishwasher to clean them, and they won't have crusted-on food."

"If I put it face up, I have to grab the part people put in their mouths when I empty the dishwasher." She arches a challenging eyebrow.

I shrug. "So, wash your hands before you empty the dish-washer. What's the big deal?"

"The big deal is that I'm pretty sure my guests don't want my hands all over their cutlery."

I open my mouth to respond, but a male voice interrupts us from the front of the house. "Hello?"

Ashley gives me an annoyed once-over before leaving the kitchen. I change out the cutlery, putting it in the dishwasher the right way.

A minute later, she returns with a man wearing jeans and a hoodie. He looks to be around our age, early thirties. Jealousy hits me that this might be her boyfriend.

"Carter, this is Ester's son, Neil."

"Hey, Neil, nice to meet you." I put a spoon in the cutlery container and step over, hand extended.

Neil squeezes my hand in his firm grip, then turns his attention back to Ashley, smiling widely. "Show me what's up."

"Over here." She turns and heads to the fridge, and Neil's attention shifts to Ashley. Her ass, to be specific. I recognize the appreciative gleam in his eyes.

The whole time Ashley explains the state of her fridge, he watches her in a way that tells me he's hoping to accomplish more than fixing her fridge by the time he leaves. He's probably going to ask her out.

All the muscles in my arms and chest tighten as I watch, and I realize I'm irritated by his interest in Ashley when I have no right to be.

I could've had Ashley six months ago if I'd wanted to. And even if that weren't the case, it's not as if I've never been rejected before. Usually, if the woman I'm interested in isn't available for one reason or another, I move on. No biggie. I'm not the kind of guy who stresses over things I can't control. I keep moving forward.

"So, Neil. Is this what you do for a living? Fix fridges?" I put a knife in the cutlery holder with a little more gusto than necessary.

Ashley's head whips in my direction, giving me a look like *Why are you being so rude?*

Neil sizes me up, then glances between Ashley and me. One corner of his mouth lifts the smallest amount, and he meets my gaze, male challenge shining through.

He thinks I'm competing with him? He doesn't have this situation figured out. I'm not jealous. I already had my shot with Ashley, and I wasn't interested—end of story.

"Nah, I'm just doing my mom and Ashley a solid. I'm the owner of the largest custom home builder in the state." He puffs his chest out with pride.

It was a shitty thing for me to say. Neither of my parents had big, important jobs, and they gave my siblings and me a good life. Now I feel like a dick.

"Impressive, good for you." I turn my attention back to cleaning up the kitchen, appropriately chastised.

My phone buzzes in my back pocket, and the buzzing continues, and continues, and continues. Given the frequency of the messages, it must be from my family group chat. I wipe off the counter and the dining room table, then say to Ashley, "I'll meet you in your office when you're done. Good to meet you, Neil."

"Same," he hollers from behind the fridge.

I go up to my room to grab my laptop, figuring I'll check in on work while I'm waiting in Ashley's office.

It's a cozy, welcoming space with wood bookcases and a matching desk at the far end of the room. A large window behind her desk looks out over the front yard and the strategically placed evergreens. Snow hangs heavy on their branches, and the sun reflects off it, causing me to squint when I look outside.

Once I'm seated on the sofa, I pull my phone from my pocket to see what's going on with the Russell clan.

> Mom: Carter - I'm starting to plan the festivities for Christmas and want to know when you're arriving.

> Brynn: You mean you're not bringing some random girl to spend Christmas with us this year?

Go figure, my little sister starts in with her snarky comments.

> Tre: Has hell frozen over?

And there's my older brother chiming in with his shit.

> Brynn: More likely, there's no one left in Manhattan for him to choose from.

> Tre: Hey, he's in Vermont now.

> Brynn: Fresh new hunting ground.

> Mom: Cut it out you two. I'm just trying to see how many people to cook for.

> Dad: Carter, answer your mother so this constant dinging on my phone will stop.

> Tre: Put it on silent like I've shown you a hundred times.

I shake my head and chuckle while I type out my reply.

> Sorry to disappoint, just me this year.

> And Brynn, there are still a few women in Brooklyn I haven't dated. ;)

My family's comments don't annoy me—they're right. I normally have a different woman with me every year at Christmas. But unlike in years past, I haven't been eager to move on to the next one since my last breakup.

Most people only see an easygoing, charming playboy when they look at me. But I've got more layers. No one has ever bothered to look deep enough. Sometimes I think my family believes I'm the superficial one, but I'm starting to think I'm picking the wrong women.

After I send my message, I put my phone on silent, determined to finish some work so I can start on whatever Steph and Doug need checked off their list.

Another half an hour or so passes before Ashley joins me in her office. I glance away from my screen, and it's clear from her sour expression that something has happened.

Chapter Seven

ASHLEY

"What's wrong?" Carter shuts his laptop and stares at me.

How he can tell that I'm out of sorts, I have no idea.

"Nothing is wrong."

His eyes remain on me as I cross the room, making my way to my desk. I grab my laptop and set it on the table in front of him before walking to one of the bookshelves.

"Is the fridge toast or something?"

"No, Neil fixed the fridge." I grab the holiday candle, the scent of berries and cloves wafting up my nose.

"What is it then?"

"It's nothing. Just drop it." Blood rushes to my cheeks, and they're probably redder than all the Santas.

I grab the lighter off my desk and light the wick of the candle before bringing it over, setting it next to my laptop on the coffee table. I'm going to need some zen vibes to deal with this man and all the tasks we have to complete. I sit on the couch beside Carter.

His closed laptop rests on his lap. "Did Neil do something

41

inappropriate?" His voice is laced with... something. I'm not sure what though.

"Not exactly."

"Well, what exactly did he do then?"

I recognize the note to his voice now for what it is—restrained anger.

I sigh. "He came on to me, and I turned him down, but he kept pushing." I shrug. "I was just uneasy, that's all. He didn't do anything wrong. I embarrass easily. I don't like uncomfortable situations."

When I glance at him, he meets my gaze, and I'm pretty sure we're both thinking back to that night we went out on a date and my reaction to what happened.

"Do I need to go kick his ass? Because I will."

Appreciation warms my chest. "No, Carter, you don't need to kick his ass. He's clear on the fact that I'm not interested."

His shoulders relax a bit after I tell him I'm not interested in Neil. Which is annoying, given how he made it clear he wasn't interested in me this past summer.

"Why don't you like him? He's an okay-looking guy, seems like he's successful." Carter shrugs, but his nonchalant action belies the interest in his eyes as he waits for my answer.

"I had this traumatizing night with this guy six months ago, and I'm not eager to relive it."

The corners of his mouth tighten. Our eyes lock, and I wait for him to say something. "Let's just get this over with," he says.

I open my laptop and type in my password, refusing to glance his way. "Get what over with?"

"What happened on our date."

I don't look at him as I open my email. Regardless, my face heats from remembering that night with him. The most humiliating night I've ever had.

"You made your feelings clear. There's nothing to talk about." I click my sister's email in the long list of junk emails from companies I swear I've already unsubscribed from.

Carter sighs beside me. "I apologized. I don't know what more you want from me."

With a huff, I slam my laptop shut and put it on the coffee table, shifting to face him better. "You acted like you wanted me, then once I was half naked, you pulled the 'chute. Said you couldn't do it." I use air quotes around the words couldn't do it. "Do you have any idea how humiliating it is to be all in, practically naked, and then you pull away and look at me with disgust in your eyes while you reject me?"

I'm not someone who sleeps with a lot of guys, and the fact that it was our first date and I was already willing to go to bed with Carter shows how much of a connection we shared. Or I thought we shared. I was the only one who felt that way.

"I wasn't rejecting you!" He gets up off the love seat and paces on the other side of the coffee table.

"No? What would you call it then?" I cross my arms and sink back into the sofa.

"I told you that night—it had nothing to do with you."

"And I told you that was BS."

He pushes a hand through his dark hair. "You've gotta understand... I've been best friends with your sister for more than a decade. And you look identical to her. When I got you into bed and started undressing you, I looked down, and all I saw was Steph. It felt weird. Wrong. Not only is she my friend, but she's my other best friend's fiancée. I freaked out for a minute."

"I am *not* my sister!" I hop off the couch, leaning over the coffee table toward him. "Do you have any idea what it's like to have a twin sister who looks exactly like you? Especially one who is a celebrity? Everyone thinks you're the same person just because you look alike. But we couldn't be more opposite.

Steph craves attention and loves being in the thick of things, whereas I don't. I've spent a lifetime trying to get people to see that we're not the same. We're our own people. Can you imagine what it's like to be constantly compared to your sibling?"

His shoulders drop, and he loses some of his defensiveness. "Yeah, I can actually."

"Sure, you can." I roll my eyes, sure he's saying it to placate me.

"My older brother was an army ranger and before that, a football star—the kind of guy who's always gone after what he wanted and succeeded, without fear. I looked up to him so much growing up. Then there's my little sister, who's the baby of the family, plus the only girl, so she could never do any wrong. I never really felt like I fit in, so I became the comedic relief. Now that's all they see when they look at me, so I keep the act going."

His expression is earnest and genuine. It pisses me off that some of my anger slides away at his admission and vulnerability.

I clear my throat. "I guess we both have our issues then." I plop back down on the love seat.

Carter walks around the coffee table and sits beside me. "I really am sorry for how I made you feel that night. It wasn't my intention."

Nodding, I swallow hard. "Thank you. I just felt so stupid. The rejection stung."

He frowns. "I never would have taken you back to my place—hell, I never would've let Steph and Doug set us up in the first place—if I'd known that was how I was going to feel. But Steph's been going on and on about how amazing her twin sister is for as long as I've known her, so when they tried to set us up, it seemed like a good idea. I'm sorry I hurt your feelings."

"Let's just put it behind us. We have to work together to get all this stuff done for the wedding, so it's probably good we had this talk, but let's not bring it up again."

"Onward and upward?" He arches an eyebrow and gives me a charming grin that I know has won him more than a few ladies.

"Something like that." I grab my laptop off the coffee table, signing back into my computer.

My sister texted me late last night to thank me again for being willing to work with Carter to get everything done for the wedding. She knows what went down between us and knows it's not exactly comfortable for me to be around him.

"Steph sent an email last night with a list of all the things we still have to do."

Carter looks at the list on my computer screen. "I thought she said there wasn't that much."

The list is longer than I expected, but I don't think it's anything we can't handle. A lot of it is just following up with vendors, which should be easy enough.

The biggest job looks like it will be picking up the chairs, which are about an hour away. I'm tempted to ask Steph if we can remove that from the list and find a rental company that will deliver, but I know how she fell in love with those particular chairs. They're antique gilded chairs she tracked down. They have incredible detail, and she thinks they'll look amazing in photographs if her wedding pictures get shared by the press. She wants everything to look luxe. So, I guess Carter and I will have to play moving crew to get them.

Despite my sister's lust for opulence, the wedding itself is small, which is why I'm able to host the ceremony and a small reception at the B&B.

"At least we get a meal out of it." Carter points at the screen, where one of the items on the list is that we have to do the final tasting to approve the meal.

"Mmm. That will be good. Anna is a wonderful cook."

"You know her?"

I nod. "She runs her catering business out of her house, and I've been lucky enough to attend a few events she's catered. The food is always amazing."

"Looking forward to that one then. Do you think it's easiest if we divide and conquer most of this stuff? To get more done?"

I'm irritated that all I feel as a response to his question is disappointment that we won't be checking these off together. But that's ridiculous. My whole plan was to avoid this man as much as possible throughout the wedding events. Then again, that was before we went from best man and maid of honor to wedding coordinators.

"Yeah, that sounds great. Give me your email address, and I'll forward this to you, then we can decide who's doing what."

Over the next twenty minutes, we go through the list and assign the tasks. There are still a few things we'll need to do together—picking up the chairs, the meal tasting, and Steph wants me to okay the fit of Carter's tux when he goes to try it on. Though I'm sure the man can handle that one on his own. He manages to dress himself every day, and I begrudgingly admit that he does a good job. Maybe she doesn't trust him not to swap out what he picked for a bright blue tuxedo with ruffles as a joke.

The only task that makes me uncomfortable is trying on her wedding dress to make sure it fits properly. She had her high-end designer ship it here a few days ago. If I try it on ahead of time, there's still time to get a minimal amount of alterations done in town. One of the benefits of us being twins is that we're still the same size and similar body shape. Still, I never thought the first time I'd try on a wedding dress, it would be my sister's dress.

I'm closing my computer when someone yelps, then a pained groan rings through the house. Carter and I exchange a confused look and jump off the love seat to investigate.

The moaning sounds as if it's coming from the staircase, so I head in that direction. When we reach it, we find Nick arched over at the bottom of the stairs with one hand on the railing, his other hand on his lower back. His skin looks clammy, and his face is contorted in pain.

"Nick! What happened? Are you okay?" I rush over to him.

"My damn back," he grumbles and winces.

"Did you fall?" Carter glances at the curved staircase, then at me.

"Nah, just lifted my leg to go upstairs, and something gave way. It's not the first time and won't be the last."

He's breathing hard and clearly in pain. I feel horrible. "What can we do?"

"Can you help me up to my room? I have some medication, and I need to lie down for a day or two, then I'll be fine. I'll take a heating pad too, if you have it."

"Of course." I gesture for Carter to help support Nick's other side. "All right, put your weight on us while you walk up the stairs. Go as slow as you need."

We make slow progress up the stairs, Nick cringing and biting back a few curses with every step. Worry settles into my chest. I know he'll be fine, but I hate seeing him in pain. He's my favorite guest right now.

About halfway up the stairs, Carter starts talking in what I think is an effort to get Nick's mind off the pain every time he shifts his weight to move up to the next stair. "Don't think you'll be running any races anytime soon."

Nick stops all forward movement at Carter's comment. "Nick?"

His face pales, and his shoulders sink. "The reindeer race is today. I won't be able to participate." He sags a bit in our arms, and Carter and I use more strength to hold him. "I was really hoping to win that money. Have a few things that need fixing at my place, and the prize money would've gone a long way toward that."

"I'm sorry, Nick," I say.

Carter's tipped-down lips say he feels as bad as I do. Then his eyes light up, and he nods at me as if we're in this together. What is he thinking?

"What if I try to win it for you?" Carter asks.

I mouth "what the heck" to Carter.

Nick's eyes widen, and he turns to me before giving Carter all his attention. "You'd do that?" The relief in Nick's voice almost brings me to tears.

"I can try. No guarantee I'll win." He shrugs at my questioning look. We have a lot on our plates without him taking part in Santa Fest.

"Carter, what do you know about racing reindeer?"

"How hard can it be?"

He's delusional, drunk on Christmas cheer, but I have to admit, the confidence turns me on.

Chapter Eight

CARTER

I'm not sure what I expected when I offered to fill in for Nick at the reindeer race, but being stuffed into a Santa suit, put on a pair of skis, and dragged behind a reindeer isn't what I envisioned.

Ashley is talking to the coordinator and letting him know that I'll be racing in Nick's spot, so I pull my phone out of the pocket of my Santa pants and pull up my family's group chat.

I chuckle and take a selfie.

Mom: I'm afraid to ask, but you mean this literally, don't you?

Sure do. Just think, you'll be able to brag to your friends that your middle child is this year's winner of the reindeer race.

Dad: Good luck. Don't get hurt, or you're getting a lump of coal in your stocking, because I'll have to listen to your mother worry until she sets eyes on you when you get here on Christmas Eve.

I chuckle at my dad's comment and notice Ashley approaching, so I slide my phone back in my pocket. When it vibrates a second later, I know it's likely my mom, not impressed by my dad's comment.

Ashley hands me a racing bib. "Are you sure about this?"

The line between her brows tells me that Ashley is concerned for me, which is... surprising. And progress, I guess. When I first arrived, I'm pretty sure she wanted to neuter me.

"It's worth a shot. I feel bad that Nick won't be able to participate. At least if I win, I can give him the ten thousand dollars, and he'll be able to fix up his place."

She studies me, tilting her head.

"What?" I shift in place. I don't usually get uncomfortable with anyone's attention being on me, but the way Ashley is looking at me feels different.

"It really hasn't even dawned on you to keep the money for yourself if you win, has it?"

My forehead wrinkles. "Why would it? I wouldn't be doing this if it weren't to win the money for Nick."

She studies me again, and I'm pretty sure she's shocked. I'm slightly insulted that she thinks I'd actually keep the money. What kind of person does she think I am?

I don't have time to think about Ashley's assumptions

about my character because a voice comes over the loud-speaker, instructing all the racers to go to the setup area.

"Well, good luck, Santa. Stay safe." Ashley pats the fake belly jutting out of my abdomen.

"Thanks." I pull the racing bib over my head, and Ashley helps me tie it up because it's not easy for me to move while wearing this big belly and Santa costume. I can't even reach my sides.

With her nearness, the scent of her perfume wafts over to me. It's woodsy with a hint of something that reminds me of cranberries. Feminine with a definite winter undertone.

What the hell? Why am I thinking about the smell of her perfume like that?

"You're good to go." She steps back.

I nod then head over to where the other racers are setting up. As I put on my ski boots, I try to remember everything Nick told me.

Bend forward at the hip.
Butt out behind you.
Center your weight.
Head level with the reindeer's back.
Knees close together.
Yank on the rope, not the reins, if you want him to go faster.
Hold. On. Tight.

I was feeling confident, but as I look around at my fellow racers, it's clear to me that they take this race seriously. You'd think a bunch of Santas would be jolly and happy. But all I see under the white beards are eyes full of steely determination and competition.

The race is held on a street parallel to Main. Snow that was brought in covers the shut-down road. Crowds line each side of the street, families dressed in their winter gear, kids sucking on candy canes while holiday music blasts from nearby speakers. As with everything in Mistletoe Falls, the atmosphere is festive and light.

At least for everyone not participating in the race.

One of the race organizers leads me to my spot at the starting line, and I get my first look at Nick's reindeer, Sparkles. The name isn't giving me much confidence as I look into his enclosure, but he looks big enough.

"We're going to win this, aren't we, Sparkles?"

He huffs through his nose, the cold air clouding in front of him.

It takes another few minutes to get everyone organized, and I use the time to build my confidence.

All my pep talks are wasted when one of the organizers brings me a helmet.

"Is this really necessary?" I ask him.

He laughs and walks away.

Unease grows in my stomach, but I remove my Santa hat and replace it with the helmet, then I click my boots into the skis. I'm a snowboarder at heart, but thank God, I did that race with my siblings and their partners last Christmas, where we swapped skis and snowboards. If I can ski down a hill, I can ski now. Maybe not as well as snowboarding, but good enough to win this race.

I make my way to the starting line, beside the unit where Sparkles is contained, and pick up the reins and the rope that's attached to his harness. The reindeer huffs at me as though he's eager to get this thing started.

In a moment of trepidation, my stomach sinks, and I wonder whether I may have bitten off more than I can chew.

But seriously, how fast can these things really go? They're not thoroughbreds or anything.

Chapter Nine

ASHLEY

"C'mon, Carter! Go! You've got this!" I clap and jump up and down.

If he ever heard me cheering this loudly for him, I would certainly deny it, but as soon as the race started, I couldn't help but root for him. I tell myself it's only because I want Nick to win that money, but I'm pretty sure I'm lying to myself.

Carter starts the race strong, neck and neck with another racer for the lead, but as the race continues, Sparkles falls behind. Carter pulls on the rope attached to the reindeer's harness, and Sparkles picks up the pace, growing closer to the lead racer.

Then Carter wobbles. He brings his torso up to find his balance, then his legs twist and both skis pop off his boots. He goes from riding to being dragged behind the reindeer.

I gasp as another reindeer almost stomps on Carter, flying by them. The other racer misses him, but it's too late. Carter is first on his back, then on his front, his white beard yanked away by the friction of the snow. He's dragged another five feet until he finally releases the reins, and Sparkles gallops on without him.

I run toward Carter lying unmoving in the middle of the road, face in the snow. By the time I reach him, several other people have gathered around.

"Excuse me. Excuse me," I say, pushing through. "Carter, are you okay?" I drop to my knees beside him, unsure whether I should roll him over.

He lets out a groan and rolls onto his back. "That didn't go as planned."

Despite what just happened, he's smiling. I don't know him all that well, but from what my sister said and how he seems, it feels like that's so Carter.

Then I notice the cut and road rash at the corner of his right jaw. He must've turned his head to the side when he flopped onto his front.

"You're hurt." I reach out with my mittened hand then pull it back, not wanting to hurt him.

He works his jaw and suppresses a cringe, moving himself up.

Cheers ring out farther up the road, and we watch as a sea of people gather around the winner of the race. The people who had been surrounding us trickle away to join the celebration, knowing Carter is essentially okay.

"Damn. I feel bad I didn't win that money for Nick." He's frowning, watching the celebration ensue with his legs pulled up and his arms wrapped around them.

"You shouldn't feel bad. Most people wouldn't have even offered to try."

He turns to me, and his eyes are soft and happy. "Careful, Ashley. If you keep talking like that, I'm going to assume you don't think I'm a total douchebag anymore."

I roll my eyes, but my cheeks heat. Hopefully my blush is

masked by the wind chill, which is already making my cheeks cold. "C'mon. I'll patch you up back at my place."

* * *

As soon as we arrive home, Carter insists on telling Nick the bad news before he'll let me see to his injury. I ask him to meet me in my en suite, where I keep all my first aid stuff.

I've got everything on the bathroom counter, and I'm just finishing washing my hands when Carter walks in.

"How did Nick take the news?" I ask.

"Fine, actually. Said he appreciated me giving it a go."

"You sound surprised."

He shrugs. "I figured he'd be disappointed. He could just be high on painkillers, or he felt bad when he saw my injury, and that's why he doesn't care."

"Would you stop? You did your best."

His usual stupid cocky grin spreads across his face. "That's two." He puts up his fingers. "There you go, giving me another compliment."

I nod toward the vanity. "Just get up on the counter so I can fix you up. You're too tall for me to do it with you standing."

He puffs his chest out a bit. "Three." He puts up three fingers. "You're on a roll now."

"Carter..."

He holds both hands up in a placating gesture. "Okay, okay." He hops up on the counter, still in the Santa suit minus the beard and the hat.

The suit has seen better days after being dragged through the snow, but I don't see any rips or tears. I'll make sure to wash it for Nick.

I soak a cotton pad in hydrogen peroxide, moving in front

of him. His legs part, and I slide in between. It's oddly intimate, being this close to him again.

"This might sting a little." When I gently dab at his wound, he hisses through his teeth, so I pull back. "Sorry, did I press too hard?"

He shakes his head. "Believe me, my pride is more wounded than my chin. Just caught me off guard."

"I literally told you it was going to sting."

"If I told you I was going to punch you in the gut, then did it, you'd still react to the pain." His blue eyes hold my gaze.

"Fair enough," I grumble, then get back to cleaning the wound.

He sucks in a breath, and his jaw tightens every time I press the cotton pad down, but he never draws back. He watches me tend to him, and I push away the feeling of being the center of his attention.

Remember how horrible he made you feel.

That thought should help me ignore the tug I feel toward him, but it doesn't.

I clear my throat and toss the cotton pad in the garbage. "I'm going to put some ointment on it now that will help it heal and prevent infection, then I'll dress it." Hopefully, Carter doesn't notice my voice quivering.

"All right."

This might be the quietest I've ever seen Carter. After I grab the ointment, I lightly press some on the wound. It's not terrible and should only take a week or two to heal if he takes care of it properly.

He continues to fix his gaze on me, and finally, it's time to put on the bandage. It's going to be tricky, given that he has facial hair, and I'm assuming it won't be pleasant to take off when he needs to redress it, but it is what it is.

"You should only have to wear this for a couple of days until it starts to heal over, then you can take it off." I lean in and press the large bandage gently around the edges, making sure the wound is covered.

His breath on my face causes me to notice how close we are now. I glance up, meeting his cerulean gaze. Our eyes lock and hold, the space between us pulling tight with tension.

Thank God for his fake belly between us, or I'd be tempted to break all distance between his legs. We breathe each other's air for only a moment before I step back.

Carter's hand wraps around my wrist. "Thank you."

He's looking at me as he did the night of our date, before all the shit about Steph and how we look identical. Earlier in the day, when he looked at me as though he was interested, I desperately wanted to explore this thing again, but he's already fooled me once. If I let him do it again, he'll make me the fool.

So I step back, and Carter's hand falls off my wrist. "No problem. I have to get downstairs to prep dinner, so I'll see you later."

I don't wait for him to respond. Instead, I bolt from the bathroom, not even bothering to clean up the supplies strewn across the counter because there's no way I'm falling for Carter Russell's games again.

Chapter Ten

CARTER

Ashley avoids me for the rest of the day and barely says a word to me at dinner, instead engaging in conversation with all the Santas seated around the table. Every time they say something about me or the race, she changes the topic. She leaves the table early to deliver Nick's meal to him in bed, and I don't see her for the rest of the night.

By the next morning, the wall I thought was falling has been rebuilt. She barely engages me in conversation, except to tell me what wedding items she'll be working on this afternoon.

She can pretend that something didn't pass between us in her en suite yesterday, but I was there too. Something definitely did. And fuck if it didn't surprise me. I thought this woman could barely tolerate me, but I also thought I couldn't be attracted to her, that I'd always see her and think of Steph, but that's changing the more I'm around her.

If I didn't think she'd slap me, I would have leaned in and kissed Ashley last night.

It just would've confused us both. Although I'm

annoyed, it's probably best that she's giving me the cold shoulder and reestablishing our boundaries. Steph seemed to understand my dilemma when I explained my reasons to her, but I don't think she'd let me off so easily if I did it a second time.

After breakfast, before I left the table, Ashley let me know that we have the tasting appointment this evening. She scheduled it after the guests' dinner. Apparently, they're all heading out tomorrow morning once the Santa Fest wraps up.

I spend the day catching up on work and knocking a couple of things off the list for the wedding. It mainly involves phone calls and emails confirming that one thing or another will be dropped off next week in time for the ceremony.

Because I'll be eating with Ashley at the tasting, I skip dinner in the dining room, opting instead to stay in my room and stream some of the shows I've been watching. I head downstairs about ten minutes before we're due to show up at Anna's place, and Ashley is waiting for me by the door, already dressed in her coat and gloves.

"All set?" she asks.

When I nod, she doesn't say anything else, turns, and heads out of the house. I trail behind, wishing we could get back to that moment in time when things weren't as tense between us.

Once I'm seated in the passenger seat, I decide to confront her about what happened yesterday. When we talked about our bad date from six months ago, it seemed to lighten things up, so maybe it will do the same this time around.

"I'm sorry if I made you uncomfortable last night."

Her hands grip the steering wheel tighter. "It's fine."

"It's not fine if you're going to avoid me from now until I leave. I thought we were getting to a better place."

"And how was that?"

I shrug as we turn onto Main Street and pass all the shops

decorated with lights and holiday decor. "I don't know. Friends?"

She glances at me with a slight tilt to her lips, and I realize I've tensed up, waiting for her reaction.

"I don't know what that was yesterday, but I promise it won't happen again," I say.

"I don't know what that was either," she grumbles. She flicks the blinker on her truck and turns down a side street. "Let's just forget it ever happened, okay? But from now on, you're tending to your own wounds."

A laugh erupts out of me, and she seems surprised by it. "Fair enough."

Ashley turns the truck into the driveway of an older brick bungalow. The giant evergreen on the front lawn is draped in Christmas lights and could pass for the annual holiday tree downtown. We follow the large candy canes that line the path to the front door.

Ashley rings the doorbell as I try to stay a respectable distance away—a friend zone between us.

A woman in her forties opens the door. She's dressed in jeans and a red sweater, hair pulled back, with a green apron that says *Resting Grinch Face* on it.

"Hey, Ashley, come on in. I was sorry to hear that your sister and her fiancé won't be able to make it tonight." Anna backs away from the door, and Ashley and I step inside.

"Their loss is our gain. This is the best part of being able to do all this wedding stuff for her."

She smiles at Ashley and turns her attention to me. "And who do we have here?"

"I'm Carter. The best man."

Anna takes my offered hand. "Good to meet you. Well, come on in, you guys. I'm just putting the final touches on the appetizers and salads."

She leads us toward the back of her home. The house is

decorated more for someone twenty years her senior, but it has a cozy, lived-in feeling.

I'd assumed we were heading to the kitchen, but we bypass it, and she leads us out the back door and into a small building behind her house. Even from outside, I catch a scent of something cooking, and whatever it is smells delicious—my mouth waters. Once we're inside, I'm surprised to find a modern, somewhat industrial kitchen.

"Wow, I feel like I just walked into a five-star restaurant's kitchen."

Anna turns and smiles at me with pride gleaming. "I added this onto the house about five years ago. It lets me get things done more efficiently and gives me room to hire a few people to help with prep when I have a big event booked. Plus..." She gestures behind where Ashley and I stand side by side. "It allows me to host potential clients without making them feel awkward because they're sitting at my kitchen table, watching me run around prepping their food."

I turn and see a doorway, so I walk toward it. It's a decent-sized room with pictures on the wall of different meals I'm assuming Anna has created. There's a table in the center of the room and big windows along one wall that look out over the backyard. The darkness outside prohibits me from seeing much, but I can make out a forest in the not-too-far distance, so I'm sure the view is killer in the daylight.

"You two can hang your coats on the hooks on the wall. Have a seat, and I'll bring the first course out shortly."

Ashley and I do as instructed and take seats across from each other at the table.

I struggle to strip my gaze away from her thin gray sweater and the way it hugs the curves of her chest. I tell myself it's just because I'm a man, and she's a woman. I'd notice it regardless of who was sitting across from me. It's only an observation. It doesn't mean I like it.

Liar.

I lean over the table a bit and keep my voice down. "I don't know what she's making, but it smells good. I feel like Steph and Doug did us a favor putting this one on our plates." I realize what I just said and chuckle. "No pun intended."

She smiles with an amused expression. I'm relieved to find that we seem to be back in the space we were in before things got weird again. I hope we can stay here this time.

"I told Steph that a tasting wasn't necessary, but she insisted."

"Do you think we're going to be able to get everything done?" I lean back in my seat.

"I don't see why not. Have you heard from either of them?"

I shake my head. "Doug isn't much of a phone talker. I figured you might have heard from Steph."

"Steph's probably just busy on set." Her words don't match her tone. "I'm starting to wonder if the most challenging part of having this wedding is going to be getting the bride and groom here."

Without thinking, I reach to take her hand to reassure her, but I stop myself, pulling my hand back and resting it on my thigh. "Don't worry, they'll be here. There's no way they're going to miss their own wedding."

Anna walks in carrying our first course, and although I want to continue having Ashley to myself, whatever Anna is bringing smells so good, so I'll forgive her. "All right, you two, we're going to start with the three appetizers and salad that the bride and groom picked. If there's something you don't like, or you don't think is working, let me know. We can either scrap the dish altogether and pick something else, or I can make some adjustments to the recipe."

"It all looks and smells wonderful," Ashley says when Anna sets the tray on the table.

"Anna, I have a feeling I'm going to be asking you to marry me by the time the night is through." I sit up straighter, starving since I skipped dinner.

She puts her hand on my shoulder. "Sorry, Carter, I've been happily married for twenty years."

"The good ones are always taken."

"Oh, I don't know about that." She winks at Ashley and walks toward the door. "I'll be back to take the plates and bring out the main course."

There are two white plates on the end of the tray, so I hand one to Ashley and set the other in front of me.

"Ladies first." I gesture toward the food.

"Such a gentleman." Ashley takes one of each appetizer and sets it on her plate.

"Only outside of the bedroom." I wink, and despite her eye roll, a quiet giggle escapes her. It feels like a small victory, and I like it, but I'm not going to examine why.

"Should we try the same ones at the same time?" she asks after I plate my own.

"Sure, you pick first."

There are little label cards on the tray, and she leans forward to read one of them. "I'm going to try the bacon-wrapped dates first."

I pick up the date. "On the count of...three, two, one..."

We both shove the small app into our mouths and chew. The savory flavor of the bacon mixes perfectly with the sweetness of the date, and we hum in approval.

"Oh my gosh, that's so good." Another sound of pleasure slips out of Ashley, and this time, my dick takes notice, straining against the zipper.

I clear my throat and shift in my seat. "So good."

We eat the other two apps—which are just as delicious as the first—and start on the salad.

"Nick was saying all the Santas are leaving tomorrow. Your

B&B is going to feel empty without them. Do you have more guests checking in tomorrow?" I spear my salad with my fork.

Ashley tilts her head as she finishes chewing. "You talked to Nick today?"

"Thought he might be bored and could use the company, so I visited with him for a little while. He's feeling much better. Should be able to get out of bed tomorrow for check-out." I shove the first bite of salad in my mouth and stop myself from moaning in pleasure. I didn't realize a salad could taste this good.

"I didn't sell the rooms for the week leading up to the wedding. I wanted to get the place ready without having to worry about making sure my guests were taken care of."

"That's kind of you to give up that income for your sister and Doug."

She shrugs. "She'd do the same for me."

"True enough."

The entire time I've known Steph, she's only ever spoken highly of Ashley, hence why I agreed to the fix-up between Ashley and me in the first place.

"So, is owning a B&B everything you thought it would be?" I continue eating my salad.

"Pretty much. I love getting to know my guests beyond just a name and credit card number at check-in. I always enjoyed it when my parents hosted families around the holidays or had everyone over for a big family dinner. So, the idea of hosting people in my home, even strangers, appealed to me."

"Did you always know that's what you wanted to do?"

She shakes her head and covers her mouth with her hand while she finishes chewing. "No. I used to work at a resort in Florida, an hour from where I grew up, but it just wasn't for me. When I first got the idea of owning a B&B, I did a lot of searching around online, figuring it might be easier to buy one from someone looking to retire or leave the business, rather than starting from scratch. I found the one here, and after a visit with my parents, they agreed to co-sign the loan for me to buy it."

"Wow, that's a real vote of confidence." I smile at her, happy that it sounds as though she's got a good family, just like mine.

She nods. "Good, but scary. The last thing I want to do is to mess up their finances because I fail."

"From what I can tell, things seem to be going well for you."

Ashley chuckles, and the sound makes a warm feeling spread across my chest. "There was a steep learning curve the first year, but these past two years have been much better."

"Well, good for you for taking the risk and going after what you want. It's really admirable and brave." I mean it because it's so easy to work for a company and have the security that comes along with it. To go on your own can be rewarding, but it takes guts.

"Thanks, Carter." My name off her lips does something to me that I'm not ready to examine too closely. "What about you, do you like your job?"

I sigh and lean back in my seat, having finished my salad. "That's a hard question to answer."

Her forehead wrinkles. "How so?"

I pause for a beat, deciding how open I want to be with Ashley. We may not have been on the best of terms when I arrived in town, but it's clear to me that she's a caring person who treats other people with respect. I don't think for a second that she'll belittle or judge me, so I decide to tell her the truth.

"I have a great job—fancy title, good salary. It's one I worked hard for. But for the past year, it's kind of felt like not enough." Just saying the words makes me feel like a bit of an asshole.

"Meaning you want more success?" Ashley finishes her last bite of salad and sets her fork on her plate.

I shake my head. "No, meaning I think I want to do something else entirely. Something that, by most people's standards, wouldn't be as impressive."

"If that's what you want to do, why don't you just do that?"

I groan and push both hands through my hair, staring at the ceiling for a beat, before looking back at Ashley. "I worry I won't be as successful, make as much money as I do now. I think I worry about what my family will say and think. I've worked so hard to get where I am. To throw that all away has to be a stupid decision, doesn't it?"

She tilts her head. "Depends what you consider stupid—working at a job you dislike your entire career just because you're worried about what people will say if you don't, or taking a chance on yourself and risking failure."

I chuckle. "Feel free to tell me what you really think."

Her cheeks redden. "I'm sorry, I'm not trying to be judgmental."

"Maybe I'm not brave like you." I arch an eyebrow.

Ashley laughs, and I note the difference between her laugh and her sister's. Ashley's is throatier, as if she doesn't want the entire room to notice her. How many times did I scan the tables around Steph after she'd laugh to make sure we weren't bothering anyone?

"I'm really not judging, I swear." She holds both hands up in front of her.

"It makes me feel ungrateful... to get everything I thought I wanted and still not feel fulfilled."

"What would your second career be?" She leans over the table, chin propped up by her fist. It reminds me of the date we went on and how engaged she was over dinner. Ashley takes on a conversation with intrigue and makes you feel as if she has all night to hear you babble on.

"I'd open my own consulting business. Help small business owners with their IT issues. Set up storefronts for them, provide delivery modules, and offer other solutions that make them more streamlined and professional, more able to compete. The idea of helping small businesses is much more appealing to me than working in corporate America and helping these giant corporations. I think I'd like seeing the impact my work is having."

"That sounds awesome, and I personally think you should go for it."

"Said like a true entrepreneur."

She flutters her eyelashes. "Well... I do believe in pursuing your dreams."

"Want to loan me some of that confidence?"

Our eyes meet and hold. That familiar tension from the bathroom the other night steadies between us.

Anna comes back into the room. "Okay, tell me the truth? What did you think? The dates? It's always the dates."

I clear my throat, and Ashley straightens in her chair, stripping her eyes off me.

As Anna clears the plates before bringing us the main course, I allow myself a moment to consider what it would be like to quit my well-paying, secure job and start my own business. I've handled my money well, and I have enough savings to get me by for a while, as well as enough to get a business off the ground.

The only thing holding me back is fear.

One thing is for sure. I'm going to have to decide sooner or later. This feeling of uncertainty and the looming decision hanging over my head feels like a guillotine.

Chapter Eleven

ASHLEY

"I'm so sorry, I don't know why it's not working." My cheeks grow hotter as I try for the fifth time to print out Nick's receipt—another damn error.

"That's all right. You have my email address. Just send it along when you can."

I give him a wan smile, but his suggestion is probably best over him continuing to stand there while I silently freak out, embarrassed by how unreliable this checkout process has been lately.

"Sounds good, Nick. I'll be sure to send it along as soon as the system is back up. I hope you enjoyed your stay again this year. I'm glad to see that your back is feeling better."

"Are you kidding me? I feel like I'm twenty years old again." He twists from side to side, demonstrating, and one of his white bushy eyebrows lowers and raises when he winks. "I'll see you next year. Already made my reservation."

I'm so thankful to have faithful guests like him. He's been a guest every year since I bought the place. "I look forward to it. Have a safe trip home."

He nods and walks toward the front door, trailing his luggage behind him.

Nick was the last of the guests to check out, leaving a strange kind of silence in his wake. For the first time since I bought the B&B, it'll be void of guests for a while—except Carter, but he's not really a guest, is he? I certainly don't plan on waiting on him as if he is one.

To combat the quiet, I bring my laptop into the great room and turn on *Christmas Vacation*, my favorite Christmas movie, to serve as background noise while I work out the issue with the reservation system. Guests must pay for their rooms upfront, so I'm not concerned about payment, but I do need to fix this issue. It makes me look pathetically unprofessional.

"Damn it." My entire platform for reservations is down once again.

"That's not very holidayish."

"Is that even a word?" I snap, whipping my head around to see Carter coming into the room. He's wearing a pair of jeans and a navy-blue sweater that deepens the color of his eyes.

"Whoa, bad day?"

"Sorry... I'm not feeling especially merry right now."

"What's wrong?" He sits on the couch, leaving a foot between us.

"My reservations system is down, and I wasn't able to check Nick out when he left. I'm not sure what the issue is though. There always seems to be an issue."

He nods toward the laptop on my thighs. "Mind if I take a look?"

The stubborn part of me wants to say I can figure it out on my own, but I think back to what he told me about his job and what he'd really like to be doing, and I figure he's the perfect person to help me. I hand my laptop to Carter.

He clicks the mouse pad a few times. "What's the web address for the B&B?"

I tell him, and he opens the browser and types it in. He scrolls through the site for a minute, humming to himself. It's cute, and I shamelessly watch him work a little longer. Then another hum comes out, and I'm not sure if this hum is of approval or disapproval, and suddenly I'm self-conscious about the choices I made for the website. It's not the best, most modern website, but my guests have never complained, and they can navigate it well.

He clicks to the backend of my reservation system and performs several actions I can't follow. His gaze veers to me. "You don't have to watch over my shoulder the entire time."

"Sorry." I relax back into the couch and decide to watch Chevy Chase put up his Christmas lights.

I'm not sure how long it takes him because I get into the movie, but he places the closed laptop back on my lap. "Fixed."

"Really?"

He nods. "Yeah, it wasn't anything major. Just something that got messed up during an update that was pushed out this morning. Should be good to go now, but if you have any more problems with it, let me know."

A huge relief washes over me. It would have taken me so much more time and money to overhaul the site.

"Thank you, I really appreciate it." I open my laptop and poke around to check that everything is working. It is.

"Don't trust me, huh?"

I quickly look at him to argue that's not it, but he's grinning. And god, he's so attractive. I've been pushing away the part of me that wants him since the minute he arrived in town. "That's a loaded question."

He chuckles. "I want to ask you something, but I don't know how you'll feel about it..."

"Well, that's *definitely* a loaded statement."

"I don't want to overstep, but it's about your website."

I cross my arms with the urge to be defensive and defiant to mask my embarrassment. "It's not the best thing in the world, but it does the job."

"See, no one likes IT people. You think I'm already insulting you."

I draw in a deep breath and exhale it slowly. "What is it?"

"I wondered if you'd trust me to develop a new one and show you where I think I can make some improvements. No pressure to move it over or anything, but your feedback would be helpful to me. You know, if I do go into business for myself, I'd appreciate feedback on what services you might find helpful and how much you would be willing to pay for them."

The negative part of me says he's using the excuse of his new venture when in reality, he thinks my system is shit and wants to give me a handout. That he's couching his offer to help by wrapping it up as me helping him, when really the opposite is true. But the truth is, I would love to update my website, and if I can help him out at the same time, it's a win-win. I'd be stupid and bullheaded if I don't take him up on the offer.

"All right, you have yourself a deal."

He nods. "Cool." Then he turns his head toward the TV. "This is one of my favorite Christmas movies."

I can't fight the grin that spreads across my face. "Me too!"

"It kind of reminds me of when my whole family gets together during the holidays now—pure chaos."

I smile, picturing Carter in the middle of all the chaos. "Wish I could watch it all, but I have to turn over the rooms and get the bedding into the wash."

Carter glances back at the screen. "But the best part is coming up. Chevy Chase is going to go for a toboggan ride."

He chuckles. When I don't say anything for a beat, he does. "What if we both watch the rest of the movie, then I'll help you do whatever needs to be done in the rooms?"

His offer surprises me, but maybe it shouldn't. Carter's been offering a helping hand since he arrived—with the fridge, with the wedding, with Nick, and now me. Maybe he isn't who I thought he was.

"Are you sure you don't mind?"

"'Course not. Watching a holiday movie is always more enjoyable when you do it with someone else." There's a glimmer of something in his eye, and if I didn't know better, I might mistake it for interest.

I shake off the thought. We're keeping things platonic. "That's true. Do you want me to make some hot apple cider or hot chocolate?"

"Oh... hot chocolate, please. Any chance you have marshmallows?" He bites the corner of his lip, and oh god, he looks sexy.

No. No, Ashley. Not sexy. Not at all sexy.

I playfully scoff. "Any good B&B owner has marshmallows on hand for hot chocolate. Especially in Mistletoe Falls."

He laughs and stands from the couch. "C'mon, I'll help you get it ready, then we can relax for a bit before we work."

While we prepare the hot chocolate, we chat easily about Santa Fest and how empty the house feels. Ten minutes later, we're back in the great room with blankets over our laps and our hands wrapped around warm mugs filled with hot chocolate and marshmallows, watching the movie.

Carter laughs especially hard during the tobogganing scene, and I can't help but look over and take him in. His head rocked back, his smile so big. A foreign feeling presses against my sternum as I admire him.

I could stay all night and play movie after movie, watching

his reaction. Then I remember my plans for tonight, and guilt washes over me. I hadn't intended to tell Carter about them, let alone invite him along. But I might enjoy myself more if he came along.

Before I talk myself out of it, I blurt, "I'm going to a holiday dance at the community center tonight. Would you want to go?"

He faces me and blinks a few times, clearly surprised by my invitation.

Oh God, why did you ask him, Ashley? He doesn't want to go.

"Not, like, with me," I rush out.

"No?" he asks, and there's a pique in his tone that suggests he might not have said no if I were asking him on a date.

"No, just because I feel like I can't let you just stay here and miss all the fun." I shrug as if my invitation isn't for any reason other than being polite.

"Yeah... of course." His eyes hold mine, and I try to appear as if my heart isn't racing. "I'd love to go. Sounds like fun."

"There's a catch," I say.

"Always is. Let's hear it."

"You have to wear a holiday sweater. It can be funny, an ugly sweater, or whatever. It just has to be on theme. If you don't have one, we can find something in town this afternoon."

A slow smile spreads across his face. "You have no idea the family I come from. I have the perfect thing."

"You mean you just happen to have a holiday sweater with you?"

It *cannot* be charming. I *can't* find Carter charming. It's one of those odd things about someone that you tell your friends after the breakup. Like, he had a holiday sweater, isn't that so weird?

"'Tis the season." He winks.

I ignore the way my belly swoops. "We're leaving at seven."

"I'll be ready."

We both turn back toward the TV and watch the rest of the movie in silence.

At three minutes to seven, I hustle down the stairs to meet Ashley at the front door.

I was surprised when she invited me to the dance tonight. Is it possible that she's forgiven me fully?

As expected, Ashley is already waiting for me, coat and scarf on, fuzzy red earmuffs over her ears. She takes one look at my sweater and bursts into laughter.

God, the sound of it makes me want to puff out my chest as if I'm some superhero because I made her laugh. One thing I've realized about Ashley is that she never laughs to be polite. If she laughs, it means you've done something to earn it. And for whatever reason, that makes me feel pretty damn special.

"Nice sweater." Her grin makes her eyes sparkle.

I look at my chest where there's a big Santa head, and underneath, it says *Where My Hos At?*

"Thanks. What are you wearing under all that?" The words come out weighted with innuendo, something I didn't intend, at least not on a conscious level. She's made it really clear that I blew my chance at having anything with her six months ago.

"You'll see soon enough. It might blow your mind actually." And she turns toward the door to leave.

Images of her in red lace and garters fill my mind. Which I'm sure isn't what's under her coat.

I follow her out to her truck and climb inside. The night air is crisp, and snowflakes float down to the ground, swirling up around the tires of the vehicle in front of us. It's a quick drive to the community hall.

We follow the car in front of us into the parking lot, and Ashley finds a spot even though the lot is almost full. I insist on paying for the tickets when we go inside, something Ashley tries to argue with me about, but I don't back down. Eventually, she says a reluctant "thank you" and stops arguing with me about it.

When we walk through the double doors, the first thing I notice is the large Christmas tree in the far corner, decorated with lights and what looks like paper decorations. Loud music pumps out through speakers set up in every corner. I don't recognize the song, but it's upbeat, and there's a smattering of people on the dance floor. This must be an adults-only dance, because there are no kids running around.

Food and drink are set up along one wall, and round tables are on the opposite side of the room—some full, some with only a person or two sitting at them. There's a small stage about three feet up from the floor on the far end as well.

"C'mon, let's hang our jackets up," Ashley says. She nods toward our right and leads me to a rolling coat rack.

I grab a hanger and motion for her to remove her jacket.

"I can hang it up myself." Her forehead wrinkles.

"Despite what every woman on a dating app might tell you, chivalry is not, in fact, dead." I hold out my hand, waiting for her to give me her coat.

She rolls her eyes and unbuttons her coat, then slides it off her arms. As soon as her sweater is revealed, I bark out a laugh, unable to stop myself.

Ashley is wearing the women's version of my sweater with pink sleeves rather than red. It too has a picture of Santa with the caption *Where My Hos At?* underneath.

"What are the chances?" There are tears in my eyes, I'm laughing so hard.

"As much as I hate to admit it, great minds think alike, I guess." She hands me her coat, and I hang it up.

"Apparently, we have more in common than we thought."

She says nothing, and as I hang up my own coat, I wonder if I overstepped.

When I turn back around, the two of us stand there awkwardly for a beat. It's a reminder that this isn't a date. Because if this were a date, I'd tell her how pretty she looks tonight. How I like the way she's left her hair down and styled it in waves. How her sweater hugs all her curves and makes it hard to tear my eyes off her. How I wish I could drag her over to the mistletoe I spotted in the center of the room the minute we walked in and kiss her again.

But I don't say any of that because I can't. Can't take the chance that I'll once again fuck this up. What if I'm attracted to her only to discover that I can't get her lookalike and my best friend Steph out of my head as soon as things turn hot and heavy? It's not a chance I can take, and I'll never know the answer unless I put myself out there, so I'm at an impasse.

"Want to grab a drink?" I motion toward the food and drink table.

"Good idea."

Ashley goes straight for the eggnog.

"You like eggnog?"

"I *love* eggnog."

Yet another thing we have in common. "Same. I don't understand people who hate it."

"Me neither. It's the best, and you only get to enjoy it for such a short time during the year. You have to take full advantage while you can."

"Agreed."

She picks up a large red paper cup decorated with green and red poinsettias. "Do you want the spiked version or unspiked?"

I think back to my very recent thoughts about how different I'd be acting if this were a date and say, "Unspiked please." No need for a buzz to ruin the fact that we can now be civil to one another.

She nods and fills the cup, then grabs herself a cup of unspiked eggnog too.

"Cheers." I hold up my cup, and we clink them together, then hold each other's gaze as we tip back our glasses.

"Delicious." She licks the corner of her mouth to remove a little of the eggnog.

I track the movement of her tongue, and it feels nearly impossible to strip my gaze away. When my eyes meet hers, it feels as though something shifts between us.

I quickly look away. "Do you come to this dance every year?"

She nods and sips her drink. "Yeah. It's nice because it's mostly just the people who live in town. A lot of the tourists leave after Santa Fest has wrapped up. Lets you catch up with neighbors you might not see during the long, cold winter."

"You really enjoy small-town life, huh?" I take a healthy sip of my drink. God, this stuff is even better than I remember.

"I do. I grew up in Jacksonville, which you likely know because of Steph. It was pretty much the opposite of here—hot and highly populated. It wasn't like I hated it or anything, but I never quite felt like I fit, never really was comfortable."

Her words resonate with how I feel about my job.

"You found your happy place when you moved here."

She smiles. "I did."

The more time I spend with Ashley, the more I realize that she's nothing like Steph. Not just her laugh, but she has a small scar on the edge of her hairline too. Steph dyed her hair blonde for her role on the TV show, but even before she did, I swear that Ashley's red hair glints with more gold than Steph's ever did.

But it's not just the physical stuff. It's who she is at her core. She's quieter and doesn't seem to enjoy attention. I love Steph, but Ashley is gentler, more sensitive, and more in tune with people and their feelings. She seems to prefer a quieter life than her sister and takes pleasure in the little things.

I take another big gulp of my eggnog, unsure what's going on with me.

"I'm an Oregon kid, so I've never spent Christmas anywhere warm. Always thought it would be weird, that without snow, it'd feel less like Christmas. What was it like in Florida? Did you have a palm tree as your Christmas tree?"

She gives me a bored, unimpressed look, but there's a hint of a smile to suggest she likes me flirting with her. I'm way too old for those to be butterflies I'm feeling in my stomach.

"Very original there." There's her full smile again. "Florida has a different vibe, definitely. Sucking on candy canes when it was warm or needing sunblock while we watched for Santa at the Winterfest parade didn't feel weird. But I didn't realize how much I prefer this until I moved here."

"Was Christmas a big deal in your house?" I'm not sure why Ashley seems so willing to open up to me at the moment, but I'm going to use it to my advantage.

She shrugs. "We celebrated Christmas, but it was never a huge deal around our house, you know? I always wished we had made it more of a focus. Maybe that's part of why I fell in love with this town." She sips her eggnog, and my eyes fixate on her mouth over the rim.

Get it together, man, she's drinking eggnog, not sucking your dick.

"Then you'd be in shock with my family." I finish my glass of eggnog.

"Oh yeah?"

"Last year, my parents booked a resort for my entire family. We have this competition every year where we play to win our picture as the star on the tree. I won the year before last." Her eyebrows raise. "Yeah, admitting that out loud is kind of embarrassing."

I love spending every Christmas with my family. It's the one time of year everyone is in the same spot for an extended period of time. Now that Tre and Tessa have Ryah and Maisie, it's even more critical. I don't want to be the uncle my nieces don't know.

The only thing that makes my smile falter is that Faith is a part of last year's memory. Not because I'm sad she's no longer in my life, but because I wish I'd already met the right person, my person, so I can share my family's crazy traditions with them.

I push a hand through my hair. Jesus, since when do the holidays make me so sentimental and introspective? "I'm going to get a refill. You want some?"

Ashley shakes her head and holds up her cup. "Still working on mine."

I return shortly with a fresh cup of eggnog. We chat for a while longer, while some of Ashley's friends and neighbors stop by to say hello. Everyone seems really nice, but more than that, they seem to really adore Ashley. I understand why because I'm starting to adore her too.

"We need to fill out ornaments on the tree." She hastily finishes her eggnog.

"I'm assuming that's why there are paper ornaments all over the tree?"

"Yeah, it's a Mistletoe Falls tradition. They say that every year, one person who puts a wish on the tree has their wish come true."

I chuckle, but she doesn't, so I clear my throat. "Is that so?"

"I'm serious." She takes my hand, dragging me toward the Christmas tree in the far corner.

I'm too stunned to say anything, stuck on the softness of her palm in mine. Maybe it's just her good mood. I have noticed that as the night has gone on, she's coming out of her shell.

So I don't spill it, I down the rest of my eggnog and toss the empty cup in the garbage as we pass by.

When we reach the tree, she points at a small round table beside it. There are bell-shaped pieces of paper and markers scattered over it. "You write down the wish of your heart. The one thing you truly want the most. And if you do, and you put it on the tree, yours might be the one that comes true."

My eyebrows raise. "That's ridiculous."

"It's not. Mrs. Wilkinson wrote down that she wanted her cat to make a miraculous recovery, and he did. The vet told her the day before that he only had less than a week to live. Explain that." She crosses her arms in the cute way she gets all defensive when she's trying to prove me wrong.

"Easy. The vet was looking at another cat's chart? The cat found the will to live?"

She rolls her eyes and grabs a piece of paper and a marker, shoving both into my chest. "Whether you believe it or not, write down your wish. You've got nothing to lose, right?"

She has a point, so I take the paper and marker, walking to the other side of the table to write down my wish. Nothing comes to me.

I lean over the table, one palm pressed to it, the other holding the marker, considering what my wish really is. If I could make a wish and know it would come true, what would I wish for? To start a successful business? Sure, that's important to me.

Across from me, Ashley scribbles something on her piece of paper. I'm so tempted to peek and see what she's written.

The wish of my heart...

What does that even mean?

I quiet my thoughts and close my eyes, telling myself to picture what I would want if I could have anything. Slowly, an image forms. It's blurry at first with no defined edges, then it slowly comes into focus.

The marker slips from my grasp, rolling along the table.

"What's wrong?" Ashley asks, eyebrows knit with concern.

I'm not telling her of all people.

The picture I just saw in my head was Ashley smiling at me from across a room I've never been in, which wouldn't be a huge deal if she weren't also wearing a wedding dress.

Chapter Thirteen

ASHLEY

"Carter, are you okay?"

The man looks like the Ghost of Christmas Past just came for a visit.

He pushes a hand through his thick dark hair, working his jaw, the bandage on the corner crinkling. "Yeah, I'm good."

An awkward chuckle falls from my lips. "Do you have everything you ever dreamed of and want for nothing?"

I meant it as a joke, but he doesn't laugh. Instead, his eyes are steady on me, and something in his gaze unsettles me. "There's definitely something I want."

I nod slowly, but his eyes still don't leave me. "All right, well, I'm going to go put mine on the tree."

I step away from the table, away from the awkwardness of this exchange, and walk to the far side of the tree, where my wish won't be front and center for Carter to see. I find an empty branch and wrap the ribbon around it so that my bell dangles nicely.

When I come back around the tree, Carter is still staring at his blank piece of paper as if he's puzzled.

He glances over. "Would you mind grabbing me some more eggnog?"

"Sure, I was just thinking I want some more too."

I give him a small smile and head back over to the food and drink table. My dentist waylays me, and I take a quick minute to chit chat with her before politely excusing myself.

As I approach the tree again, I watch Carter put the cap back on the marker and set it on the table. Then he goes over to hang his paper bell on one of the branches.

I commit to memory where he hangs his because I'm so curious what he wrote—an urge to sneak back later and read it takes over, which makes me a terrible person. I deserve a lump of coal in my stocking.

He turns away from the tree, and I try to appear completely normal, as if I wasn't spying on him a little. At first, that same look is on his face as when he was deciding what to write, but then his charming smile transforms his face, and he steps away, breaking the distance between us.

"Thanks." He takes the cup from my hand, and our fingers brush.

Our gazes come together, the invisible string between us pulled tight.

Carter's mouth opens, and I'm desperate to know what he's about to say, but Ester approaches from the side, dragging us both from what I feel was going to be an essential moment.

"Merry Christmas, you two."

We both mumble Merry Christmas.

"Good to see you again, Carter. How are you enjoying your visit to Mistletoe Falls?"

Carter recovers faster than I do, turning to bestow his usual grin on her. "It's a great town."

"You know, I do have a room available at the inn now that the Santas have left town." Her statement hangs, and Carter looks at me as though to gauge whether I want him to stay at my B&B or not.

Panic twists in my stomach at the idea of him leaving.

He must see something in my expression because he turns back to Ester. "I appreciate that, but I'm already settled, and it makes it a little easier now that Ashley and I are having to help with the wedding."

She turns to me, concern in her gaze. "Oh? What's going on?"

I explain to her what happened with my sister's schedule and how Carter and I have stepped up to ensure things go smoothly for their big day.

"Well, I'm sure you both have it handled. I heard Neil was able to fix your fridge."

"He was. Thank you again for sending him over." I manage to hold the smile on my face. No mother wants to hear that her son was a little too pushy when it came to asking for a date.

"Oh, he was more than happy to help. He was supposed to come tonight, but something came up."

I watch Carter take a long drink from his eggnog, and when he pulls the cup away from his mouth, his lips are pressed into a hard line.

"Well, I really do appreciate his help," I say.

Ester turns to Carter, and he schools the severity of his expression into a more neutral one.

"Will you be participating in the festivities later?" Her head cocks to the side.

Carter's gaze flicks to me, but I shake my head, unsure what she's referring to. "What festivities are those?"

"The Santa Strip Tease. It's a new thing this year. Holiday music plays while a Santa strips down to his underwear, but to keep the song going, money has to be donated every twenty seconds. All the money goes to the local elementary school."

I already know what Carter looks like in a Santa suit, but now I'm picturing what he'd look like out of one. Of course, my cheeks betray my thoughts, heating so hot I feel as if I'm in front of the fireplace.

Carter must notice it too because he chuckles. "I'm not sure, Ester. We'll have to see."

She faces me. "You know, women can participate too. It's for a great cause."

My eyes widen, and my cheeks get even hotter. "Um… I think I'll pass. I'll donate though."

She opens her mouth, and I fear she's going to press this issue, but thankfully, the universe is looking out for me because my phone buzzes in my back pocket. I pull it out and see that it's my sister.

"Excuse me, I'm just going to step out to take this." I hold up my phone and rush out into the hallway, not wanting to miss this call. "I've been trying to get a hold of you for days," I answer as I step out of the room.

"I know I'm sorry. The schedule has been brutal since we're trying to get this done before the holidays. If I'm not on set, then I'm sleeping. How's it going? How's everything with the wedding coming together?"

I love the excitement in her voice, so I set aside my irritation that she hasn't gotten back to me. "Great, no worries. We've done the tasting already, and your meal is going to be mouthwatering. We're picking up the chairs in a few days, and I have an appointment tomorrow with the seamstress to try on the dress and get any small alterations done."

"Oh, Ash, you're the best. Thank you so much, we couldn't do this without you guys."

My chest warms at the appreciation in her voice. "Of course. What good is having a twin sister if you can't have her step in at the last minute to arrange your wedding?"

We both laugh.

"And how is it with Carter? Managed not to kill each other yet, I take it?" She's trying to mask her trepidation with humor, but I know her too well.

I hate the idea of Steph being concerned that her big day will be ruined because Carter and I can't manage to put aside our differences. Though I'm not even sure we have many differences anymore. Since I've had to spend more time with Carter, I've realized that he's not all that bad. In fact, he isn't anything like I thought he was.

"Don't worry about us. We're getting along fine. He might not be that terrible of a guy after all." With the toe of my boot, I kick at a crack in the old flooring.

"I told you! You know I wouldn't be BFFs with an asshole."

"Yeah, well, you can't blame me after my first experience with him."

There's silence for a second. "Ash... do I sense some interest in your voice..."

My back goes rigid. "What? No way. I will not put myself in that position again. Not a chance."

"If you just—"

"Steph, it's not happening."

"Okay, okay, I'll leave it alone."

"Thank you. Now, is there anything else you need me to do? Mom called me earlier today to make sure I could handle everything on my own—wanting to come and take it over, I'm sure."

"No surprise there." I can practically see Steph rolling her eyes.

Our mom is a little type A and tends to manipulate her way into taking over any project she offers to *help* with. Hence, Steph made it clear when she started planning her wedding that Mom's help wasn't required because she'd hired a wedding planner.

"I'm surprised she hasn't hopped on a flight already and shown up on your doorstep," she says.

"The only reason she hasn't is probably because she hates the cold so much."

We both laugh.

"True. She's likely trying to limit how many days she must spend in the *frigid north*," Steph says.

We both cackle. It's how my mom always refers to where I live... *How's the frigid north? Is it getting warmer yet in the frigid north? Are you even able to get flowers to grow in the frigid north?*

"All right, I have to get back on set." There's a sadness in her tone, and I feel her. I miss her so much. "I can't wait to get there. Thank you again for everything."

"What are twin sisters for? Love you."

"Love you too. And listen..."

"Don't even go where I know you're going," I say.

"Just if something develops between you and Carter, I say go for it. He really is a good guy. I promise."

"Steph, I swear to—"

"Love you, bye!" She hangs up before I can continue my tirade.

I shake my head and slide my phone in the back pocket of my jeans. I stand in the hallway for a moment longer, thinking about what she said. Part of me wishes I could be more spontaneous and see where these feelings for Carter take me, but the other half of me is too afraid of being embarrassed and hurt again. Isn't one rejection from the man enough? Why would I set myself up for two?

When I return to the party room, Carter is sitting alone at one of the tables. He's such a social guy that seeing him solitary seems... off.

He hasn't spotted me yet since he's looking contemplatively into his cup of eggnog.

Gary, the local butcher, is hanging his paper bell on the Christmas tree, and I wave.

I look into my cup. It's three-quarters empty, so I knock back the rest and walk over to the food and drink table to get the two of us another glass.

I rock back and forth to the beat of the music as I ladle the buttery yellow mixture into the cups. I'm feeling light and at ease. Maybe I should forgo this cup, but it's Christmas time, and it's been so stressful lately, I deserve to let loose a little.

Now I realize that to walk over to Carter, I have to pass the Christmas tree, and I fully intend to sneak a peek at what he wrote on his paper bell. Maybe it's a little sneaky. I could ask him, and he'd probably tell me. But then he might ask what I put on mine, and I'd feel like I had to tell him, which is an absolute no.

Once I've poured both cups, I make my way along the wall, watching to make sure Carter doesn't notice me. I don't want him to know I'm being a snoop.

I go along the back of the tree to where I saw him hang his paper bell. It takes me a second to locate his, but when I do, I step closer to read what he wrote.

MY WISH IS THAT MY VISION WILL COME TRUE.

I frown. Not what I was hoping for. What is his vision? It must be about the business he wants to start.

Disappointment shouldn't be what washes over me, but it does, and it makes me wonder what I was hoping I would read. Why did I want to snoop in the first place?

"Got you another." I set the paper cup in front of him and sit to his right.

"Thanks, appreciate it. I'm assuming it was Steph?"

I nod and sip my drink. "Yup. Just checking in."

I watch everyone dancing in the center of the room, and

for the first time, I want to join them, which is odd since I've never once danced at a community event. I've always been too self-conscious about how people would be watching me.

I catch Mrs. Mitrovski shuffling over toward our table. I divert all eye contact, hoping she'll decide to find another place to sit. "Oh god, we need to get up from this table right now."

"Why?" Carter glances around as though he's not sure why I sound so panicked.

Once he gets sucked into a conversation with Mrs. Mitrovski, he'll understand. She's a lovely lady, but it's impossible to extract yourself once the conversation starts. You'll politely tell her you have to go, and she'll acknowledge it, then bring up some other topic.

"Are you going to introduce me to your handsome friend, Ashley?" Mrs. Mitrovski sits next to Carter.

"You'll see," I say out of the side of my mouth, then relax into my seat because I'll be here for a while.

Chapter Fourteen

CARTER

My eyes stay on Ashley out on the dance floor, dancing and jumping around, looking as though she's having the time of her life to "Rockin' Around the Christmas Tree."

If I didn't know better, I might think she's drunk, or tipsy at the least. To be honest, I feel the same, which makes no sense since we're drinking non-alcoholic eggnog. I guess we're drunk on Christmas cheer. It's probably the only thing that's kept me at this table for so long with Mrs. Mitrovski—the fact that I've been able to zone out so much.

Ashley was brilliant to leave with the excuse of dancing—to escape the prison that is a conversation with this woman. I wish I'd jumped out of my seat when Ashley tried to warn me. Not only does Mrs. Mitrovski keep the conversation going for far too long, but she barely lets me get a word in edgewise. I think she might be more interested in a captive audience than she is in scintillating conversation.

"And that's when I told him, I said, 'Alexi, if you insist on cutting down that tree in the front lawn, don't be surprised if your clothes are waiting for you on the front porch when you get home.' I mean, can you imagine? Cutting down a fifty-year-old tree because it's blocking your view of the neighbor you want to spy on? It's ridiculous. You'd think that after thirty years of marriage, he'd know that—"

Thankfully, she's cut off by the earsplitting sound of feedback from a microphone. It's worth the hearing damage to put an end to this conversation.

Everyone turns their attention to the stage, where a woman in her fifties with graying hair cringes. "Sorry, everyone. I wanted to let you know that we're going to start the Santa Strip Tease in about five minutes. Anyone who's planning to take part, please meet me beside the stage now."

She sets the mic back in its holder, and the music comes back on.

Before Mrs. Mitrovski can say anything, I push my chair back. "Sorry, I've gotta go."

She looks me up and down. "You're doing the Santa Strip Tease?"

Fuck, am I? I just wanted to get out of this conversation.

"I mean, thirty years, but we planned this cruise for next year—" she starts in again, and I see another half hour at this table.

"Yeah, I am. Sorry, you can tell me all about the cruise later." I hope my smile masks the fact that I will never corner myself into a conversation with her again.

"Well then, I'm going to get my pocketbook out. Go now." She shoos me away with her hand.

I didn't really plan on participating, but it's given me the perfect excuse to get out of this conversation. Plus, it's for a good cause, right?

At the side of the stage, all the men are standing around. I introduce myself, and the woman from the stage, Monica, explains how it will work, echoing Ester's explanation from earlier.

"If there's a specific song you want to dance to, I can see if we have it." She eyes me up and down.

I'm a little embarrassed to admit one of my favorite holiday songs, but what the hell. "If you have Justin Bieber's 'Mistletoe,' that'd be great."

She chuckles quietly. "All right, I'll see if we can get that for you. There's a bin full of Santa suits over there. Find one that fits well enough and put it on. You can use the restroom to remove your other clothes. We're going to start in a few minutes."

I nod and go over to the bin. It doesn't take long to find one that will fit, and I rush off to the bathroom to change. When I return, I chat at the side of the stage with the other three guys who are participating. One man looks as though he's probably in his seventies, the other might pass for twenty-one, and the third guy appears to be in his late thirties or early forties and has a beer belly on him that would rival the actual Santa Claus's. I'm pretty sure he's not using a fake belly like the rest of us.

I thought for sure I'd be nervous, but for whatever reason, I'm not at all. I can be extroverted when I want to be, but I would have thought I'd have *some* nerves about stripping in front of strangers. More importantly, Ashley.

Monica returns to the stage, and she looks nervous for some reason.

She taps on the microphone and clears her throat. "Hi, everyone. Before we get started with the Santa Strip Tease, I have an announcement to make. It's come to my attention that someone mislabeled the eggnog. The punch bowl labeled non-alcoholic is actually the eggnog with alcohol, and vice versa." She bites her lower lip. "Apologies to everyone. If anyone needs a ride home, both Rick Springer and Ester Layton have volunteered to drive you home safely."

I laugh. Well, that explains the buzzed feeling I have. I

search out Ashley, and her eyes go wide in horror, but then she shrugs it off, making me laugh even harder.

"Now, to get on with the fun stuff. Let the Santa Strip Tease begin! First up, we have Nathan." She gestures to the side of the stage, and the guy in his early twenties steps up, chest puffing, full of bravado.

If I had to guess, he's probably been dipping into the alcohol-laden eggnog too. His cheeks are flushed, and his smile wide and proud.

"This one is for all you MILFs out there!" he shouts before the music starts.

"I Saw Mommy Kissing Santa Claus" plays, and the echo of laughter rings throughout the room.

He first removes his Santa hat, then slowly unbuttons his belt. Monica calls for a donation as the song approaches the twenty-second mark, and a woman in her fifties steps up and passes her some cash. It goes on like this until the song ends and Nathan wears only his Santa pants. He didn't work fast enough to get the entire costume off.

Monica thanks him for his participation, then calls Bob with the big beer belly up onto the stage. Bob doesn't seem to have any qualms about stripping.

"Santa Baby" plays. He pivots his hips around in a circle, and a very enthusiastic woman steps up in front of the stage, hooting and hollering. I have no idea whether it's his wife or girlfriend, but she's clearly going to be the one who donates the most for him.

Bob grins at her and unbuttons his Santa coat. The woman hands Monica money every time the song reaches the twenty-second mark, and the performance threatens to end if there isn't a donation.

When the song is over, Bob hops off the stage with an agility and grace I didn't see him having and kisses his biggest fan. The people in the room cheer, but Bob and his woman walk out the doors, the rest of the Santa suit and his clothes forgotten.

Monica turns her attention to me and the old man beside the stage and calls Arthur up. I have to help him up the stairs, but once he's on the stage, his entire countenance changes as if the crowd's cheers buoy him.

I'm not familiar with the song, but I think it might be called "Backdoor Santa" based on the lyrics alone, which makes it even funnier watching Arthur slowly remove his clothes to the jazzy tune. The crowd is more into it than any of the other participants thus far. My competitive juices flow, but then I glance into the crowd and see Ashley with her hands over her mouth, laughing hysterically, and I realize that the only person I want to impress is her.

In fact, the more I look at her, the more the realization dawns. I want... *her*. Ashley. I was an idiot six months ago. She's nothing like her sister. Now, if they were standing side by side, I wouldn't look at either of them as being an extension of the other.

The audience's cheers crescendo, and I blink a few times, dragging my gaze from Ashley to the stage. Arthur has finished his dance and managed to take his entire costume off in the time he had. I never realized how short most Christmas carols are until now.

I help him back down the stairs, my heart thumping since I'm next.

Monica calls me up on stage, introducing me. Finally, the nerves hit me through my boozy brain, and I swallow hard. But when the music starts, I keep my gaze locked on Ashley's broad smile, and somehow the nerves drift away.

I gyrate my hips as I unbutton the red jacket lined with white fur. Hoots and hollers ring out from the crowd, and I grin. Still, I don't look around, holding Ashley's gaze the entire time I undo each button. When my fake belly slips, I pull it out entirely, twirling it over my head and tossing it in her direction. She catches it and laughs. Her smile and happiness make me feel like a superhero.

Twenty seconds is way too fast. Monica calls for a donation to be made to continue, and to my surprise, it's Ester handing Monica some cash to keep me going.

I wiggle the jacket off my shoulders, revealing my bare chest and abs, loving the way Ashley's gaze zeros in on my six-pack. The night of our date, we didn't get far enough for her to see me fully. I was still working on undressing her when I acted like an asshole and called it off. Right now, I've never despised myself quite so much because if I hadn't been an idiot and been able to see Ashley for who she was that night, we'd both know what the other looks like naked.

The jacket freefalls to the floor, and the audience roars. My fingers go to my belt, and I work my pants as donations come in every time Monica requests. My pants pool on the floor, and I step out of them, leaving me in my tight, black boxer briefs and a Santa hat.

I motion with my finger for Ashley to step toward the stage, and surprisingly, she comes, never removing her gaze from mine. When she's close enough, I take the hat off my head and place it on hers.

God, calling her up here was a bad idea. All I want to do is kiss her. Thankfully, the music comes to an end before I'm standing with a hard-on in front of half the town of Mistletoe Falls. The end of the song somehow severs the tie between Ashley and me. We both blink and step back from one another.

Monica thanks all the participants and donors for their time and announces how much money was raised, while I slink off stage and grab my clothes to change into.

When I return to the hall, I bring the Santa costume back to the bin and scan the room for Ashley. She's still out on the dance floor, enjoying herself. It's good to see her let loose, even if it is because she's been drinking all night without knowing it.

I break the distance, reaching for her and grabbing her hips, twirling her around. Her surprise morphs into excitement when she sees that it's me.

"You did so great up there!" She wraps her arms around my neck and hugs me.

Her body pressed against mine has me closing my eyes and imagining what this would feel like if we were both naked.

Just then, the song ends, and rather than another upbeat song coming on, a softer, slower one starts. "Have Yourself a Merry Little Christmas" plays, and people around us pair off to slow dance.

I pull away enough to look Ashley in the eyes. "Care to dance?"

She holds my gaze with a small flirty smile that makes my dick twitch. "I'd love to."

It's obvious something has shifted between us. I'm not sure exactly what or when, but things feel different even if we're both ignoring it. Clearly, she feels it too, by how welcoming she is to me.

Ashley leaves her hands around my neck, and I set my hands on her hips as we rock back and forth in a circle. I'm so transfixed by counting the gold flecks in her eyes, I realize our eyes haven't swayed from each other's.

"Did you like what you saw up there?" I ask after a few moments of silence.

"I did." She bites her bottom lip, and I almost audibly groan, wishing I could lean in and pluck it free with my teeth.

"Good."

"Good?" She arches an eyebrow. "You wanted me to be impressed?"

"That's all I wanted while I was up there."

She rubs against me with every shift of my body. I don't think you could fit a piece of peanut brittle between us, we're so close.

"Why would you hope that?" Her voice is quiet and soft, so I almost don't catch it over the music.

"Isn't it obvious?"

She shakes her head as we continue to move. "Not to me."

I've successfully led us to the center of the room. I glance up, and she follows suit, finding the mistletoe hanging above us.

"There's a reason I was dancing to Justin Bieber." I laugh. "It was fair warning."

Her gaze stays on mine, and she smiles. Then she holds her breath and waits. "Oh."

This isn't the first time we've kissed, but it's the first time we've kissed with intention. I really understand who Ashley is and what I want from her.

I bring my hands up to her face, cupping her cheeks. Slowly, so gradually, I lean in, giving her time to push me off if she doesn't want this. To tell me this is a bad idea. But she doesn't.

At the first press of my lips to hers, our kiss instantly feels different than the first time. It's night and day different. This kiss is all-consuming. Life-affirming. This kiss is the kind they write about in those romance novels my sister reads.

Slowly, I drag my tongue over the seam of her lips, and she opens for me. The moment our tongues meet, we both moan. Her fingers go into the hair at the back of my head, and she sways into me. My dick is hard between us, pressing against her stomach, and I deepen the kiss.

Our tongues glide along one another's, and the taste of her feels like a shot of whiskey on a fire, flaming my arousal higher, the heat scorching. My need to have her grows with every second of our kiss, but before I can satisfy myself, the song ends, and another high-energy Christmas carol comes on.

We pull away from each other, and our eyes hold.

"Want to get out of here?" she asks, and I love even more that she's on board with me.

"All right. Just stand with me for a minute while my dick softens. Don't want to give your townspeople more to talk about."

Ashley laughs, resting her head on my chest, and my hand instinctively goes to her back, rubbing up and down. It's not really helping me calm down, but damn, she feels good in my arms.

I scan the room for Ester, trying to think of things like evil Christmas elves running a coup in Santa's workshop, or those sad animal commercials they always run this time of year to get people to donate. Anything to get myself presentable so we can get the hell out of here and back to her place.

After a couple of minutes, I step back. "Okay, I'm good."

Ashley's gaze dips to my dick. "I like it better the other way."

Oh, she's definitely feeling her eggnog.

"I spot Ester. Let's get a ride from her." I slide my hand in hers, and she tightens the hold, much to my male pride's delight.

Ester agrees to drive us back to the B&B, and Ashley insists I sit in the front since I'm taller. I make small talk with Ester on the short drive home. Really, I'm only half paying attention because my mind is entirely on what I'm hoping will happen with Ashley in her empty B&B when we get there.

I'm not going to sleep with her tonight since she's been drinking, but that doesn't mean we can't share a bed and cuddle and kiss.

I'm shifting in my seat when Ester pulls down the drive of the B&B and brings the truck to a stop.

"Thanks again for the ride. Really appreciate it," I say.

"No problem at all." She smiles, and we both look into the back seat, finding Ashley slumped over, sleeping. "Oh, jeez."

I admire her peacefully before I disturb her. "I'll carry her in. I hope her keys are in her purse."

Ester chuckles. "Oh, city boy, she probably didn't lock the door."

Shrugging, I climb out of the truck and open the back door, reaching in and slipping my hands under Ashley's legs and behind her back. "Thanks again for the ride, Ester."

She nods and watches as I carefully pull Ashley from the vehicle, then nudge the door with my hip.

Ashley cuddles into my chest and sighs as I walk up the path toward the house. Ester is right—the door is unlocked. I turn the knob with my hand under Ashley's legs, pushing with my back to close it.

I walk Ashley up to her bedroom and lay her on the mattress. She moans and turns a few times as if she might wake up. But she doesn't and gets settled again, so I remove her boots and pull the covers over her.

Even though I want so badly to slip in beside her and spend the night holding her, I cast the idea aside. I don't want to share a bed with her unless she's invited me to, and although the dance and kiss were hot, she's in no condition to ask me. So I quietly tiptoe back out of the room.

The entire night plays in my mind as I walk to my room—the mismarked eggnog, the Santa Strip Tease, all the new townspeople, and... the wish tree. Shit, I meant to go to the tree and see what Ashley's wish was. I was vague enough in mine that no one would figure it out. As I go to my bedroom and shut the door, I kind of hope that vision returns in my dreams because it doesn't scare me as much anymore.

Chapter Fifteen

ASHLEY

I roll over in bed, squeezing my eyes shut from the dull throb stabbing my brain.

It takes me a moment to figure out why I have a headache, then I remember. The holiday dance, the eggnog, Carter on stage stripping as Santa... our kiss.

A pleasurable warm hum fills my body as if I'm reliving it all over again—God, that kiss.

It didn't even come close to comparing to the kiss we shared that night of our date. Not that those kisses were bad, they weren't. But after the kiss we shared last night, they lacked any genuine desire on Carter's part. Last night, it was filled with passion and longing and desire. His dick pressed up against me was evidence that he wanted me as much as I wanted him.

But what does it mean, if anything? I have no idea where Carter's head is. It's been great getting to know him better, and he's not the asshole I once thought he was. But did he kiss me because it meant something to him, or because he was tipsy on eggnog, and I was there?

Pushing the covers off me, I rise out of bed, telling myself not to dwell on Carter and me. Not to hang my happiness on whatever Carter's reaction might be.

When I reach my en suite, I start the shower and grab some pain medicine for my headache before stepping under the warm spray. Since I don't have guests, and no one is waiting for me to make breakfast, I'm able to take a longer shower than usual, and I fully indulge in the extravagance. I shave my legs and use my favorite body wash with a coarse hand mitt to scrub my skin.

I tell myself I'm not doing this on the off chance that Carter and I end up in bed together, but I know it for the lie that it is. Like it or not, my hopes are invested in Carter. I hope he doesn't disappoint me again.

Once I've gotten dressed, dried and styled my hair, and put on a touch of makeup, I go downstairs. Thankfully, the shower and ibuprofen chased away my headache.

As I approach the kitchen, I hear someone moving around inside it, and I draw in a big breath, trying to settle my nerves. This is the moment I'll know exactly where Carter's head is.

"Good morning," I say.

Carter is rinsing his plate in the sink. The dishwasher is open, and he's loading his breakfast dishes inside.

"Morning." He glances in my direction and gives me the briefest of smiles before turning his attention back to the dish.

He's paying attention to it as if he's performing brain surgery, and my stomach twists that we're back here again. He regrets and wishes the kiss hadn't happened.

"I made some extra pancakes." He puts the plate in the dishwasher.

I glance toward the stove, and there's a plate with a stack of pancakes. "Thanks. I appreciate it."

The butter and maple syrup are already on the table, so I make my way to the stove. Neither Carter nor I says a word as I pick up the plate, walk over to the cutlery drawer to grab a fork and knife, and sit at the table. Carter is busy wiping the counters, diverting all eye contact with me.

Maybe he's as nervous as I am about how the other feels about our kiss last night. Perhaps the best thing to do is to act normal and show him that I don't regret it.

"Did you have a good time last night?" I unscrew the top on the maple syrup bottle and pour the sweet goodness over my pancakes.

He clears his throat and turns on the faucet to run the cloth under it. "Yeah, it was a good time. Though I hadn't planned on getting tipsy on eggnog nor stripping in front of most of Mistletoe Falls."

Is that his way of signaling that he was drunk last night and that's why he kissed me?

"Yeah, me either. Well, the eggnog, not the stripping."

Neither of us says anything, and I hate how awkward this feels. I'm about to tell him when my phone rings in my pocket. I pull it out and see a number I don't recognize, but that's not uncommon these days with all the wedding stuff I've been working on, so I answer it.

"Hello?"

"Can I speak with Ashley, please?" an older gentleman's voice asks.

"This is Ashley." I glance at Carter, who's rooting around under the sink to get the dishwasher detergent out to start the dishwasher.

"This is Thomas McCleary. I hear you're the one who's going to be picking up some chairs for your sister's wedding."

I straighten in my seat. God, I hope there's not a problem with the chairs. I know my sister has her heart set on them. "Yes, is there a problem?"

"Well... I hope not. I wanted to see if you could come tomorrow to grab the chairs instead of waiting a few days. My wife is having an unexpected surgery the day after next, so I won't be here the day you were supposed to come."

"Oh, I'm so sorry to hear that. I'll have to call the place I'm renting the truck from and make sure they have one available tomorrow, but I don't think it will be a problem."

He sighs in relief. "I really appreciate it, thank you."

"Of course. If there's an issue, I'll call you back. Otherwise, I'll see you tomorrow."

We say our goodbyes, and I rest the phone on the table.

"What was that all about?" Carter asks, leaning against the counter with his arms crossed. His body language is not even close to open and relaxed.

"I have to pick up the chairs tomorrow. Does that work for you?" I'm going to need his help. Truth is, I'm hoping he'll drive the truck since I've never driven anything that big.

"Guess I'm going to have to make it work, won't I?"

Irritation flares inside me. Annoyance comes next. I'm tired of guessing where his head is. We need to be adults and have a conversation about the kiss.

"Carter, can we talk about—"

"I've got to jump on a work call." He pushes off the counter.

My hands tighten around my knife and fork as he leaves the kitchen, offering me his back. He won't even have a conversation about last night?

My cheeks heat because I feel like a fool. Apparently, I'm the only one who feels such a strong connection between us. I thought I'd figured out who Carter is, but maybe my first impression of him was the right one.

Chapter Sixteen

CARTER

I'm such a dick. I did some dickish things when I was young, but nothing this bad.

Continuing to push Ashley away this morning after the kiss we shared last night makes me the lowest of the low. But it was the right thing to do.

I set aside my laptop. I've been trying to get some work done at the desk in my bedroom for more than an hour now, but my thoughts keep returning to Ashley.

Pulling my phone from my pocket, I scroll through the text chain from my family to reread them. I woke up to it this morning. Apparently while I was having an amazing time with Ashley last night, they had nothing better to do than to pester me.

Mom: Carter, you haven't let us know if anyone else will be joining us over Christmas. Is it safe to assume it's going to stay that way?

Dad: Thought he already told us it would only be him.

Brynn: When is it EVER just him?

Tre: LOL. How many different women have we met over the years?

Brynn: I can remember at least five, but I think I have to be forgetting someone.

Tre: Mom, want me to learn Photoshop so I can erase them from our holiday pics? ;)

Mom: You two leave your brother alone.

I put the phone down, not bothering to read the rest of the texts. It's just more of the same. They're riding me about how I've never had a woman spend Christmas with us more than once.

They're busting my balls like we do in my family. Hell, I'm usually the ringleader, but the timing of it stings because last night, I was imagining inviting Ashley to spend the holidays with my family. How right it would feel to have her there, and how much it would hurt to leave her behind after the wedding, not knowing when I'd see her again.

When I woke up this morning, I was excited to see Ashley, to find out what might come of the two of us. Every minute I spend with her, the connection seems to grow. But seeing my family's messages made me question everything I thought I was feeling.

Is my family right? Is this destined to be another fling or relationship that doesn't go anywhere? I brought Faith last Christmas and look how that ended. Would I be doing the same with Ashley?

All those doubts, not wanting to ruin this thing with Ashley anymore, made me step back this morning and really consider what I'm doing, even though everything in me was ready to jump in with both feet before reading those messages.

She's Steph's sister. I can't fuck this up a second time. Then I'll be off the list for all Steph and Doug's events for good. If I never see them, never get to be the uncle to their kids, our relationship would slowly die, and I couldn't even blame Steph.

With a huff, I drag my laptop over and try to get back to work. But within ten minutes, I give up, my mind back on Ashley.

Closing my eyes, I lean back in my chair, replaying last night in my mind. How much fun we had together, how we laughed effortlessly with each other—even before we'd drunk too much of the spiked eggnog. I remember how much the people in town seem to like and respect Ashley and how everyone who leaves a conversation with her seems to step a little lighter. I can't help but think of our kiss and the way she tasted, how it felt to have her body pressed against mine.

Mainly, I can't help but think about how I've never felt like this about anyone before and so quickly. Sure, I've had relationships, but if I'm honest, the women were always more invested than I was. Most often, I could take or leave them, and I never thought long term.

But with Ashley, it's *all* I think about. When I lay down in bed last night, I kept picturing that vision I'd had of her in a wedding dress. It probably should have scared the shit out of me, but it somehow felt right. Inevitable. Which is crazy.

Then when I came back with a snarky, shitty reply this morning, the look of disappointment on her face was almost my undoing. I was the one who caused it. Again. As though I'd let her down and become the guy she thought I was.

"No. This is not how this is going to go. Not this time," I mutter.

I pick my phone up and text Ashley.

Where are you?

I heard her leave earlier. I'm assuming she must've called someone to pick her up and take her to her truck because I heard a vehicle in the driveway, then the door to the house opened and closed, and she hasn't returned. She's probably going on errands or doing wedding stuff down on Main Street.

I don't bother waiting for her reply, knowing it'll take me a bit to walk there. I grab my coat, hat, and gloves, slip on my boots, and head out.

The sky is overcast, and snowflakes are cascading to the ground slowly since there's no wind. It's not enough to accumulate—not that I'd mind getting snowed in with Ashley if it means I can make this right.

I've been walking for a few minutes when my phone buzzes in my pocket.

Why?

So I can meet you and apologize for this morning to your face.

I could have waited until she returned from whatever she's doing, but my mind hasn't been my friend, and I don't want to give myself time to second-guess what I know is right—that Ashley and I can be something good.

I like this urgency inside me to tell her now. I don't want to scare her off by coming on too strong, but I need her to know. I need to apologize for stepping back this morning.

She doesn't text back immediately, and a growl of frustration slips out of me.

Main Street comes into view as my phone vibrates again.

Fine. Apology accepted.

I'll scour downtown for her truck and every storefront to find her if I have to. A minute later, another text comes through.

My head snaps up, and I scour the buildings in front of me to see how close I am to her.

207 Main Street

Not far. I keep my phone in my hand, watching the street numbers climb higher and higher. My footsteps grow faster the nearer I get until I'm practically jogging. When I finally stand in front of 313, I don't bother to look at the building or the storefront. I whip open the door and rush inside.

Then I come to an abrupt halt.

Ashley looks the same as she did in my vision the night before.

And that's when I know that I should never have questioned my feelings for this woman because she's meant to be mine. Forever.

Chapter Seventeen

Carter barges into the seamstress's shop and stops. His gaze tracks up and down my body slowly, cataloging every detail.

I would've thought seeing me in a wedding dress would've made all the color drain from his face, but it does the opposite. He looks at me in awe, with a kind of reverence reserved for a real bride and groom.

"I'm just trying on Steph's dress to make sure it should fit her," I say a bit awkwardly since he's staring at me, and I'm staring at him, waiting for him to say something.

He still doesn't speak but walks toward me with his mouth open and his eyes wide. His nose and cheeks are red from the cold air outside.

"Hello? Carter?" I wave my hand in front of him.

The seamstress, Carla, had to go to the back to answer the phone, so it's only Carter and me.

"You look…" He shakes his head as though he can't believe what he's seeing. Then he shoves his phone in his pocket and takes both my hands. "I'm sorry for this morning."

"It's fine. I already accepted your apology. Next time, don't be a jerk about it."

He shakes his head with more force this time and squeezes my fingers. "I didn't regret our kiss. Not at all. But I can't lie, it scared me."

My head tilts. "Scared you? Am I that bad?"

Carter presses his lips together. "God no, you're incredible. I'm scared because I feel too much for you. Too soon. But that doesn't mean that what I feel is wrong. It took me a minute to realize it."

"So, you didn't feel like you were kissing Steph last night?"

"Not even close." He shakes his head for what must be the third time. "All it took was spending more time with you than one dinner to see the wonderful, nuanced woman you are." He pushes a hand through his hair. "I honestly can't believe that I ever saw you as an extension of your sister."

Something fills my chest until it is buoyant with what I think might be hope. "Carter... are you *sure*?"

I hadn't really realized how much I wanted this until this moment. Maybe I didn't want to hope and be shut down, too terrified to put myself out there again.

He cups my face. "I've never been so sure of anything. You're meant to be mine, and I'm going to prove it to you." He leans in and kisses me.

The kiss is even better than last night's because this time, I won't be left wondering what it means. This time, it means everything.

* * *

After Carla finishes pinning me for alterations, Carter and I hold hands as we walk around downtown, checking more wedding stuff off the list. It feels so good to be with him—like we're a couple. So natural, as if we've always been that way.

Tonight, we're going ice skating, something I've avoided since the first time I tried it after I moved. Growing up in Florida, winter sports were never really part of my life, and I figured out quickly that ice skating isn't the easiest skill to pick up—at least not for me. But Carter assures me that he's a pro and will help me out.

It's not a traditional ice rink that we're going to, but an ice path that runs through the forest. The route is lined with string lights, and there are vendors selling handmade goods, food, and drinks, and even a spot where the kids can sit on Santa Claus's lap. I've heard a lot of people in town talk about it before, but I've never been because of the whole having-to-skate-to-enjoy-it thing. But as soon as we arrive, I wish I'd tried harder to learn because it's beautiful.

Huge evergreens, branches heavy with snow, line either side of the path that winds through the forest. The hanging lights create a soft glow on the snow of the forest bed and reflect off the ice.

Carter and I head under an archway of red velvet ribbon and Christmas balls into what resembles a Christmas village. Holiday music rings out, and all the vendors are set up along the outside of a large circle. In the middle, tables and Adirondack chairs are set around roaring fires.

"This place feels magical." I turn to soak in Carter's reaction.

His wide ocean eyes glimmer as they bounce from one thing to the next. "It sure does. I can't believe you've never been here before."

"I know. Now I feel like I was missing out. Makes me feel like a wimp for not trying harder."

We both chuckle.

He squeezes my hand. "I'm kind of happy you didn't."

"Why?" I cock my head.

He looks down. "Because it's our first of firsts."

"First of firsts?" I giggle, and his smile grows.

"The first time we get to do something together that neither of us has done before."

My heart soars. It sounds so lovely, and I can't wait to do the next one.

"And of course I get to act all macho and show you how to skate. An ego thing, you know?"

"Oh, I know."

He places a kiss on my temple. "Let's go get our skates."

"Are you sure you want to take responsibility for my safety on the ice? I'm really not good." I stare at the skates on the counter, remembering how I could barely stand as kids were whizzing by me.

He shakes his head and hands me my skates. "Just don't break anything. Steph will kill me if you're wearing a cast in her wedding pictures."

I laugh as we walk to a nearby bench to put on our skates. Carter gets his on in record time, and I take my time tying my skates.

"Well, I see your first problem."

"What?"

"They aren't nearly tight enough. Here." He stands in front of me and motions for me to give him my foot.

He's towering over me, and I hadn't realized how much taller ice skates make someone. I raise my leg, and he holds the blade of my skate between his thighs and unties the laces.

"You must trust me a lot. One quick flick of my ankle, and you're in bad shape." I waggle my eyebrows.

He sets his eyes on me. "Believe me, you injure him, and you're the one missing out." He arches an eyebrow.

The space between my thighs tingles. His long fingers flex as he fixes my laces, tying them tighter than I had, and a quick picture of him doing this for a child, our child, comes to mind.

I mentally chastise myself because what the heck was that?

Talk about fast forwarding—I don't even know what this thing with Carter is. It's not as if we've talked about it. Why am I already casting him in the role of father to my children?

Get a grip, Ashley.

"There you go." He gently sets down my leg.

I wiggle my toes, and Carter holds his hand out to help me stand. I can instantly feel how much more stable my ankles are. "This is much better. Thanks."

He places a chaste kiss on my lips. It makes me smile, this ease with which we've fallen into being comfortable showing each other affection.

"Want to give it a shot?" he asks.

"Let's do it."

My skate hits the ice, and I immediately fall, almost taking Carter down with me.

"Try to keep one foot planted and push off with the other one." Carter holds my hands and skates backward in front of me.

I do as he instructs and take a wobbly glide forward. But at least I've found some balance, and I'm no longer falling on my ass every time I move.

"That's it, you're doing great. Now do it again and then again."

Other people whip by us, but Carter says to ignore them, don't think about how stupid I probably look. Normally, the mortification would have me packing it in like I did last time, but Carter gives me the confidence to keep going. I push off like he said and do it again and again until what I'm doing bears some resemblance to skating.

A grin forms on both our faces.

"You're doing great," he says. Carter has been so patient. "Let me know when you think you're okay for me to let go of you."

His words make me grip him harder. "Not yet."

He chuckles. "I'm not going to let go until you tell me you're ready. Don't worry."

"Did you skate a lot growing up?"

He nods. "Played hockey growing up. I was never amazing at it, but I did all right. I'm trying to convince my brother, Tre, to put my niece Ryah in hockey. I want to take her skating when I visit."

I remember from our first date that he grew up in a small town named Climax Cove in Oregon.

"He's not into it?"

Carter shrugs. "We used to have a bit of a rivalry growing up since he was the star football player, and I was into hockey."

"Do you enjoy being an uncle?"

The megawatt smile is on his face answers before he even responds. "It's the best. Ryah has such a fun personality, and I'm sure Maisie will be the same. She's just a baby, so I haven't seen her enough."

A warm smile stretches my mouth. After my experience with him teaching me how to skate, I can picture him being a wonderful uncle to his nieces.

"Do you want to be a father someday?" I feel a little awkward asking that question. I don't want him to think that I'm wondering as it relates to me, even if I kind of am.

His gaze meets mine, and it feels weighted with possibility as though he knows why I'm asking and is okay with it. "I do, yeah." Then he squeezes my hands, like some kind of promise.

I try not to read too much into it, but my heart pumps out a staccato beat.

A couple holding hands leisurely skates by us, the male in the couple glancing over his shoulder when they pass. When I see him do a double-take, I groan because here it comes. He pulls the woman he's skating with to a stop, says something to her, and she turns and looks at us before a huge smile transforms her face. And now they're coming over.

"Get ready," I whisper to Carter, who looks baffled until the couple stops right next to us.

"Oh my god, I love *Shelter Bay*!" the woman practically shouts.

"Except your hair is different," the man says.

Carter stiffens in surprise, then slowly releases my hands, shifting to my side and wrapping his arm around my waist to keep me steady.

I smile at them as nicely as I can. "Actually, I'm not her. It's my twin sister on the show."

The guy scoffs. "Yeah, okay. You look exactly like her."

Carter frowns. "Did you miss the part where she said they're twins? Identical twins?"

The man glances from me to Carter. "Listen, if you don't want to talk to some of your fans, just say so. You don't have to make shit up."

The woman tugs on his arm. "What's it like being on a TV show with Rick Selleck? He's so gorgeous. Do you think he'll be your love interest on the show next season?"

Her face fills with excitement. Here comes the bad part. I brace myself. I always feel bad when I have to burst people's bubble and make them really understand that I'm not her.

"It's my sister, honest to God."

Her eyes narrow, and her gaze tracks me up and down, taking in all my features. "You're right. You're a little curvier than she is."

"And not as pretty," the guy says.

Carter skates in front of me, as if he can block the insults. I lose balance but grip the back of his jacket, holding steady for the moment.

"What's wrong with you guys? You two don't know what the hell you're talking about. Ashley is a thousand times better." His head whips over his shoulder. "Don't tell Steph I said that."

A laugh bubbles out of me. Despite the insults these two strangers have just leveled at me, I find the humor in Carter's reaction.

"Whatever," the guy says and rolls his eyes.

The two of them skate off, grumbling to themselves, and Carter turns around, gripping my hands as he circles. It's a sexy-as-hell move. He pulls me in and wraps his arms around my waist.

"Thanks for coming to my defense."

His forehead wrinkles. "You know what they said was total bullshit, right?"

"Yeah, I know. I'm used to it."

The wrinkles on his forehead deepen. "Does it happen a lot?"

"Not quite like that, where people are that nasty, but most people don't believe me when I say I'm not Steph. It takes some convincing."

"Now I understand why you reacted the way you did on our first date. Which makes me feel even more like an asshole." The pain in his tone soothes a little of that hurt I've been harboring.

"Honestly, things like what just happened bother me less than when someone knows me and still thinks my sister and I are carbon copies of each other."

Carter kisses the tip of my cold nose. "I'm sorry I ever made you feel that way."

"I know you are. But listen, I can be a little too sensitive about it, and I probably overreacted that night. I was really into you and felt this instant connection during dinner, and I was hopeful about where things might go between us. So, when you did a one-eighty, I was embarrassed and disappointed."

He cringes and inhales through his nose, his eyes never straying from mine. "Rest assured, now that I know you better, I can't imagine why I ever saw Steph in you. I wasn't kidding about what I said to them. You are a thousand times better." Then he gives me a good, long kiss. "But seriously, don't tell Steph because she'd probably cut my balls off, and that would hurt you as well as me now."

We burst into laughter, causing me to lose my balance. My feet slip out from under me, and I grab onto Carter, taking him down with me. We end up in a tangle of limbs, laughing even harder.

Chapter Eighteen

CARTER

The next day, I'm in charge of driving the truck to pick up the chairs. Ashley is too scared, since she's never driven a vehicle this big. Not that I have any experience. I've lived in Manhattan for a long time now, so driving in general is a bit of a foreign concept to me.

But after the first twenty minutes, I catch on and feel confident.

After skating last night, we returned to the B&B and had hot chocolate and made out like teenagers in front of the fire. Though I wanted to take Ashley upstairs to her bedroom and have my way with her, I don't want to rush this thing between us. I messed up once already, and I'm determined not to do it again.

I have no reservations about sleeping with Ashley. I don't think that what happened last time will happen again. Everything in me tells me this is meant to be between us—she is my destiny. And I want to make sure we go at a pace she's comfortable with.

So I dragged my turned-on, sorry ass to my room, tossed and turned for an hour, unable to sleep until I took a shower, masturbated to visions of Ashley, and then finally could fall asleep.

Now, she's in the seat next to me, singing along to a Christmas carol playing on the radio.

"Aren't you going to sing along with me?" she teases.

"If you want your eardrums to bleed the rest of the trip, I can."

She laughs and goes back to singing.

I glance at the sky. It's supposed to snow—hard—and we're on a race to beat the winter storm rolling in.

By the time we reach our destination, the snow has begun. It's not coming down terribly hard, so if we do this quickly, we should be okay to get home.

The man who owns the chairs chats up Ashley and me as we load the chairs into the back of the truck and secure them, so they won't shift while I'm driving. I don't know what I expected these chairs to be. They're nice chairs, sure. But are they worth all this effort? I don't think so. But then again, I'm not a bride who wants her wedding day to be perfect.

By the time the chairs are all loaded and we're ready to leave, the driveway is covered in a couple of inches of snow.

We're getting back on the main road when the back end slides a little. "I'm going to have to go slow with this weather since I'm not used to driving a truck." I glance at Ashley, who is nervously biting her bottom lip. I squeeze her thigh. "Listen, it's going to be okay."

She nods, but rather than answering, she pulls out her phone. "The weather app says it's only supposed to get worse."

Five minutes later, I feel as if we're in a blizzard. The snow is falling rapidly, and even with the windshield wipers going full speed, they barely clear the glass. Not that it matters much since I can't see more than a few feet in front of me.

As we round a bend in the road, I feel the back of the

truck slipping out to the side again. Ashley yelps, and I straighten the vehicle.

My knuckles are ghost white on the steering wheel, and my heart thunders. "This is going to take us forever to get back, and it's going to be dark in a couple of hours. What do you think of finding somewhere to stick it out tonight and then get on our way again when the roads are plowed tomorrow?"

I expect Ashley to say that she has to get back to the B&B. To say that she has so much to do for her sister's wedding that she can't possibly afford to be stuck somewhere for tonight and into tomorrow. But she doesn't. She must really be scared.

Instead, she says, "I think that's smart. Let me look up where the closest place is."

Within a few minutes, we have a plan. There's a motel a few miles up the road. We'll stop there and wait it out.

Rounding the final curve in the road before the motel comes into view, I breathe a sigh of relief at seeing the glowing red vacancy sign through the falling snow. We pull into the parking lot. There are a lot of other vehicles here, though whether they had already planned to stay or the storm brought them in off the road, I don't know.

"You stay in the warm cab while I get us a room." I don't wait for Ashley to argue with me before I open the door and slide out.

Thankfully, I have my boots on, but the snow is already almost over the top of them.

I walk into the small reception area. A man I'd place in his early sixties sits behind the counter, glasses pushed halfway down his nose, a pen in hand, staring at a crossword puzzle.

He looks up when the bell dings as I make my entrance. "Goalie known for the most blocks in a single NHL game?" He arches his gray bushy eyebrow.

"Conor Nilsen," I say as I stomp the snow off my boots.

"Nilsen. Right, of course. Thanks." He writes the name in and sets aside the paper. "What can I do for you?"

"I need a pair of rooms." I didn't ask Ashley if she wanted her own room, but I'm not going to assume she wants to stay with me.

The man frowns. "Afraid I only got one room left. Storm pushed a lot of people off the roads."

I sigh. "Any chance it has two beds?"

He shakes his head. "Just the one."

I nod and pull my wallet out of my pocket. "It'll have to do then."

The man is really friendly, checking us into our room, and I leave the reception area with the key for room number thirteen. The gentleman tells me there are some vending machines in the laundry room at the end of the motel.

I slip twice on the walk back to the truck, but I manage not to go ass over tea kettle. I get back in the cab of the truck, thankful for the heat pumping out of the vents. "I got us a room."

Ashley smiles. "Awesome."

"But there was only one room available. With only one bed." I wait for her reaction, but I'm not sure what other choices we have.

"Okay, well, that's not the end of the world." She holds my gaze.

I nod and turn off the vehicle. "All right, let's go then."

We head to room thirteen, and when I swing open the door, I'm pleasantly surprised. You can never be sure what you're going to get when you stop at a motel on the side of the road, but this place is nice.

There's what looks to be a double bed in the center of the room and dark wood nightstands with a matching dresser. A relatively new TV is mounted to the wall over the dresser, and a small table with two chairs sits in the corner. The carpet is dark green with flecks of gray, and the bedding appears to be a flannel comforter coordinating with the carpet. The room is painted beige with older landscape art prints throughout the room. It's a little dated, but it's cozy and, most importantly, clean.

"This is pretty nice," Ashley says as she walks in and looks around.

We remove our boots and leave them on the rubber mat near the door.

"Are you hungry?" I thumb at the door behind me. "The guy mentioned that there are some vending machines."

She shakes her head and unzips her jacket. "I'm okay for now."

I unzip my jacket. "What do you want to do then?"

She shrugs. "Want to see what's on TV? We can relax."

* * *

Six hours later, we're deep into the Food Network's *Holiday Baking Championship*. They're doing a marathon today, and Ashley said she loves the show. Now she's turned me into a fan. Jesse, the host, is funny in a weird way with all his puns, and it's cool to see what the contestants can come up with on the fly.

"I'm going to have to tell my mom about this show. She'd love it." I toss another one of the chips from the bag on my lap into my mouth.

"Is she a baker?" Ashley asks from where she's propped up against the headboard beside me.

"Not so much throughout the year, but during the holidays, she's a hardcore baker. My sister-in-law Tessa is actually a baker. She had her own place in Manhattan for a while."

Ashley's eyes widen. "Oh wow. Remind me never to bake for either of them." She seems to think better of what she said, then her eyes widen even more. "Not that I'll ever meet them or have the opportunity to bake for them, I just—"

I quickly kiss her lips. "I'm counting on you meeting them at some point."

She blinks rapidly. "You are?"

I nod slowly. "I'm counting on a lot of things. I haven't told you because I don't want to scare you off."

The corners of her mouth tip up. "Me too."

"Yeah?" My head tilts.

"Yeah."

We hold each other's gazes for what seems like several minutes. Maybe only seconds.

Then, unsure if I should act on my instincts or not, I look away. "I think I'm going to go have a shower and brush my teeth before we settle in for the night." Nice that the vending machine had toiletries too.

I don't know what to make of the fact that she licks her lips when I say that. "Sounds good. I'll have my shower when you're done."

I slide off the bed and practically run to the bathroom before I invite her to join me. If the signals I'm reading are correct, she's down with things turning physical tonight, but I don't want her to think that's all I'm interested in, so I'm going to need her to make it *really* obvious that's what she wants.

I have a quick shower, brush my teeth, and quickly redress. She goes into the bathroom after me, and when she does, I strip down to my boxer briefs and slide under the covers.

The entire time she's in the bathroom, all I can think about is that she's naked in there. I picture her rubbing soap all over her body, but I end up tenting my boxer briefs, so I try to think of unpleasant things. When that doesn't work, I turn off the TV and roll onto my side, deciding that maybe the best thing to do is go to sleep.

But I have no luck, so when the bathroom door opens a few minutes later, I hear Ashley come back into the room. I'm facing away from the bathroom so I can't see her, but I swear she's watching me. It's as though I know everywhere her gaze travels as tingles move from one part of my body to another.

The bed dips as she sits on it, and the sheets rustle in the dark as she climbs under them. My breathing picks up its pace because her body spurs heat under the covers. It's not a huge bed, so we're close, practically touching.

Then we are touching as she winds her hand around my waist from behind and presses her front to my back. Only I don't feel the soft cotton of the T-shirt she wore under her sweater. No, her breasts are pressed against my muscled back, the points of her taut nipples dragging against my skin as she moves up to kiss my shoulder.

"Ashley, what are you doing?" The words are raw, and I'm barely holding on until she gives me the green light.

"What I hope you want to." Her hand dips down my stomach, squeezing my hard length over the fabric of my boxer briefs.

I release a quiet groan. "Are you sure about this?"

"I think the better question is, are you?"

I whip around so fast I might startle her from the noise she makes. Then she giggles. But I don't give her any time to recover before fastening my mouth on her nipple, twirling my tongue around the hard nub then biting down lightly before soothing it again with my tongue. Ashley gasps, and her hands dive into my hair, pulling at the strands.

I give her other nipple the same treatment before I'm over her, dragging my tongue down her body toward the apex of her thighs. I find heaven on earth with the first lap of my tongue through her center. Her sweet, musky taste is now my favorite flavor. Screw the sweetness of hot chocolate or the peppermint of a candy cane. Ashley is the taste I want on my tongue—always.

Ashley's back arches off the mattress as I suck her clit. Her fingers grip my hair harder, but the pain in my scalp doesn't deter me. I push two fingers into her and the noise she makes is the sweetest music to my ears. As I continue to play with her clit with the end of my tongue, I curl my fingers to hit her G-spot.

"Carter, oh my god. Don't stop," she moans.

"I don't plan to stop until you're coming on my tongue, Ash." My mouth returns to her clit, and I suck it into my mouth, using a steady rhythm to curl my fingers into her.

She climaxes in under a minute, calling out my name and grinding her pelvis onto my face. Her back arches off the bed as I commit the entire scene to memory, never wanting to forget this moment.

When she comes down from her orgasm, I work my way back up her body. I kiss her, and she returns it greedily as if she likes the taste of herself on my tongue. My erection strains between us, and god, I want to sink into her so badly. But only if she's ready. Now that she's gotten off, she may decide she wants to slow things down.

Ashley trails her hands from my hair down toward my waist, slipping her fingers around the elastic of my boxer briefs and pushing them down. "You need to take these off. Do you have a condom?"

It takes a moment for the words to work their way into my brain because all the blood has rushed to my dick because *holy shit we're going to have sex with Ashley.*

I can't believe I was ever stupid enough to push this woman away. I was a fucking idiot.

"I have some in my wallet." I roll off the bed and look for my pants in the dark. They're hanging over the chair in front of the table. I yank my wallet out and slide a condom out of it, discarding the wallet on the table.

When I reach the side of the bed again, I pull off my boxer briefs. I'm not sure how much Ashley can see in the dark, but she spends a good deal of time checking me out. It makes me puff my chest out a little because she clearly likes what she sees.

Bringing the condom wrapper to my mouth, I tear it open.

Ashley reaches out her hand. "Here, let me."

My dick twitches between us, something she notices because she chuckles. I pass her the open condom wrapper, and she pulls out the condom, crawling over to sit on her knees in front of me. Her petite hands grip me, stroking a few times. My eyes drift closed with the sensation, and my head rocks back, tilting toward the ceiling.

When I feel her grip the base and roll the condom on, I open my eyes and stare down at her. God, she's gorgeous with her red hair spilling over her bare shoulders and her eyes glittering in the dark as she looks up at me.

Once the condom is on, I kiss her and gently lead her with my body back up the mattress. I don't remove my lips from her the entire time. Not until she's lying across the mattress and I'm hovering over her. And only so I can take her in as I slide inside her for the first time.

I watch the way her eyes widen the slightest amount. The way her mouth opens, and she sucks in a breath. The way her entire body relaxes as though she can finally exhale. Gently, I rock into her, an inch or two at a time, until I'm fully seated inside her.

"God, Ashley..." I hold myself and bask in the sensation of her warm heat surrounding me. I trail my tongue from her collarbone, up her neck and to her ear. "It's official. I won't ever get enough of you."

She turns her head and licks the seam of my mouth. Our tongues tangle as I move inside her. My hips pound out a steady beat as the heels of Ashley's feet push against my ass. I take my cues from her, and when she digs her heels in, I increase my pace.

Sex has never felt like this for me—amazing physically but also so wrapped up in emotion.

I know for sure that I'm never letting this woman go.

Chapter Nineteen

ASHLEY

My heart riots as Carter moves on top of me. Everything about this joining feels so right. So meant to be.

It's silly to think like the fantasies of a teenage girl, but I can't help it. I've never felt so much like this is where I'm supposed to be.

"You feel so good," I say, truth slipping from my lips. I feel as if I'm both in and out of my body.

"Fuck, Ash, I don't ever want to stop."

My body contracts around him when he calls me Ash.

"You like that do you? Ash?" It happens again, and he lets out a low chuckle. "I want to see you."

Without warning, Carter wraps his arms around me and sits up so that he's sitting back on his heels and I'm straddling him. My hair drapes over one shoulder, and Carter gently moves it so that it lays along my back, exposing my bare chest to him.

I move over him. A moan works its way up my throat from the feel of my clit rubbing against him. I'm not going to last long in this position.

Quicker than I would like, the sensation of my impending climax builds. Carter's fingers weave in my hair as he looks up at me in what I can only think of as awe. His gaze echoes what I'm feeling—though I've been like this with a man before, it's never been like *this*.

It's like knowing that this moment is going to change the trajectory of our lives.

His hand moves to my ass, and he grinds me against him. A cry of pleasure releases, then suddenly my orgasm barrels down on me. I clench around him, pleasure twisting through my entire body.

Carter pummels up from underneath me and groans out his own release. He swells inside me and pulses until we're both covered in sweat and gasping for breath.

"I never knew it could be like that," he says, his breathing labored against the skin of my breast.

"Me neither."

Once we've caught our breath, he gently sets me on my back before slowly pulling out of me. It feels like a profound loss. He seems to feel the same based on his frown.

"I'll be right back." He climbs off the bed and disappears into the bathroom.

He returns moments later, lying down on his side, propping himself up on his elbow, and trailing his fingers over my stomach.

I stare at his handsome face, just visible in the darkness. "Your chin is healing well." Today is the first day without the Band-Aid on.

"Yup. Should be good by the wedding. Enough not to be obvious at least."

The mention of the wedding brings something to mind. It feels early to have this conversation, but the days before the wedding are ticking away.

"Speaking of the wedding... how do you want to handle it?

I mean... do you want to hide what we've been doing from my sister and family, or..." Thank God we're in the dark because my body is heating and not from the orgasm.

Carter tucks a strand of hair behind my ear and kisses the corner of my mouth. "I want whatever you're comfortable with. Given my friendship with your sister, I wouldn't have done any of this unless I thought this could really go somewhere. But I don't want you to feel pressured."

And to think that I once thought this man was inconsiderate.

He trails his finger along the edge of my hairline, and I bring his palm to my lips and kiss it. "I don't want to hide this from anyone. I want us to feel free to let this be whatever it's going to be."

A slow smile spreads across his face. Even though it's dark in the room, it somehow still lights up the space. "Then we're on the same page."

Carter shifts off his side so that he's over me again. Then we're kissing, and then hands are moving, and then we're doing everything we just finished doing again.

It's even better the second time around.

* * *

The next day around lunch, the roads are finally cleared enough for us to drive back to Mistletoe Falls. It's a good thing, but I'd be lying if I said I wouldn't miss being holed up in this place with Carter all to myself. Without the outside world and all its demands intruding.

We check out of our room and pull onto the highway. The snowbanks at the side of the road are many feet higher than they were on our drive yesterday, but the roads are clear.

"What do you have planned for the rest of the day?" Carter asks me when we're about ten minutes out of town.

I shrug. "All the bows need to go on the backs of the chairs, and they need to be set up in the room where the ceremony will take place. I have a couple other things to do around the B&B to get it ready since the first guests will be arriving in a few days."

"Think you have time for some fun today?" He glances at me quickly, his straight white teeth on display.

"What kind of fun did you have in mind?" I waggle my eyebrows.

Carter's laugh makes my chest warm. "Well, that kind of fun is always on my mind. But I was thinking maybe we could go tobogganing. I noticed a spot when we left town yesterday."

My stomach tingles with excitement. "I've never been tobogganing."

His head whips in my direction before turning back to the road. "What? Really?"

"You forget, I grew up in Florida, and I was an adult when I moved here. It's not really the kind of thing you go out and try for the first time on your own. Not at this age anyway."

He reaches across the cab and squeezes my hand. "Another first of firsts then?"

"I guess so." I'm giddy like a crushing teenage girl, but I don't care.

"Then we have to do it. How about we go home and unload these chairs and head out to the hill before it gets dark? I'll help you with the other stuff tonight."

"Sounds great." I'm excited to go tobogganing for the first time, but I'm even more excited that I'm doing it with Carter.

An hour later, we've finished unloading all the chairs, and I collapse onto one of them. "I don't know if I'll have the energy to climb up the tobogganing hill now."

Carter chuckles. "Seriously. I don't remember it being that much work when we were loading them on the truck."

"We had adrenaline rushing through our veins since we were trying to beat the storm."

"Could be. Do you still want to go?"

"Absolutely. Just let me change into something warmer first."

"Meet you back down in ten?" He arches an eyebrow.

"I'll be ready."

I head up to my room and change. Then I quickly braid my hair into two pigtail braids, so my hair won't be whipping in my face or getting tangled. Within ten minutes, I'm waiting at the front door with my snow pants on, hat on my head and mittens on my hands.

I'm not usually an adventurous person, but I'm enjoying doing new things with Carter. If this is anything like skating was, he's going to be patient and supportive. Not that I think there's a lot of skill in sitting on a sled and riding down a hill.

Carter's footsteps bound down the stairs before he comes into view. When he does, the space between my thighs tingles. He too has snow pants on and a ski jacket. He wears a navy-blue beanie and gloves. He looks nothing like the city guy he is in his daily life in Manhattan. I think I'm getting to see a glimpse of what he was like growing up in Oregon.

"You ready to—" The sound of his cell phone buzzing from his pocket cuts him off. He pulls it out and looks at the screen, frowning. "This is Carter... Hi, Ralph... Yeah, everything should have been good to go..." Carter's shoulders slump, and he looks at me, frowning harder. "Yes, of course. I'll get on a call with the team right away and get to the bottom of it... It's no trouble... Of course... I'll let you know once it's resolved." He hangs up and holds his phone in his palm at his side.

"Problems at work?" I try not to let too much of my disappointment seep through in my words.

"I'm sorry. I'm not going to be able to go. There's an issue with a big client at work, and my team can't handle it on their own."

"That's okay." My voice sounds more chipper than I feel. "I'll just start in on all the things I need to get done. It's probably for the best anyway."

Carter pockets his phone and steps forward, resting his hands on my hips. "Are you sure? I feel awful."

I set my hand on his chest, disappointed I can't feel his muscles through his winter jacket. "Of course. You go do what you need to do."

He kisses the end of my nose. "I'll make it up to you, I promise."

"You don't need to make it up to me."

"As soon as I'm done with this, yule be mine." He grins and arches an eyebrow. "See what I did there?"

I chuckle. "Very punny."

He laughs and gives me a chaste kiss. "I'll come find you when I'm done."

"Looking forward to it."

He squeezes my hips and heads back up the stairs.

But he doesn't come find me until well after dinner because the issue was more involved than he expected. I'm disappointed but tell myself it's not the end of the world.

Chapter Twenty

CARTER

I felt like an ass for having to ditch tobogganing with Ashley a couple days ago, so I've been working in secret to finish what I envision for her website. She probably thinks I've forgotten about it since I haven't brought it up since I got all her passwords and the information I needed. But I'm hoping to wow her when I present it to her. Which is in about five minutes, unbeknownst to her.

Steph and Doug are due to fly in tomorrow, so today is my last opportunity before the chaos begins and Ashley is completely distracted by her twin sister's wedding.

I told Ashley I had to work this morning, but I've been putting the final touches on everything and making sure it's perfect so that I can bring down my laptop at lunch and show her what I've been working on.

After I unplug my laptop and close it, I head downstairs to find Ashley. She's in the dining room, polishing silver. I remember her saying that Steph wanted to use some of their grandmother's serving ware for the dinner after the ceremony.

She looks up at me then smiles. "All done with your work stuff?"

"Yeah. Do you have a minute?" I hold up my laptop.

"Sure, what's up?" She sets down the platter and cloth.

"Let's go to the great room. C'mon."

We sit on the couch side by side. I set up my laptop on the coffee table in front of us. The fireplace has a small fire going, and holiday music plays through the TV. The room smells like cinnamon as always.

"I finished up working on my proposal for your website. I actually built a whole strategy on how I think you can improve your visibility online and draw in more people to your B&B. I'm ready to show it to you and see what you think."

Excitement glitters in her eyes. "Really? I thought maybe you got busy because you hadn't mentioned it."

I shake my head. "I've been working on it. Took this morning to finish it off."

She gestures to the computer. "Let's see it. I'm excited."

"All right, but remember you have to be honest with me. Tell me your honest opinion."

Ashley rests her hand on my knee and squeezes. "I promise."

I log in to my computer and pull up the new and improved Silver Bells B&B website. As I go through all the features, like the ability for her to easily add pop-ups for stay add-ons like champagne and strawberries, or upgraded toiletries, or tickets to local attractions that will help to increase each guest's value to her business, she sits quietly, taking in everything. I go through a few more add-ons I thought that she and her guests might appreciate. By the time I've spoken for ten minutes straight and am wrapping up, she still hasn't said anything.

When I finish, I can't get a read on what she's thinking. "That's about it. What do you think?"

She looks away from the computer screen and at me, face not showing any emotions until a slow smile spreads across her face. "Carter, this is amazing. I thought you were just going to redo my website. I didn't realize you were also going to improve the functionality of it and make improvements to my business at the same time."

"Did I overstep? I wasn't trying to."

Ashley squeezes my thigh. "Not at all. These are all things I've considered but had no idea how to implement or didn't think I could afford to implement them."

I shrug. "I've seen how hard you work and how much you love what you do. I just wanted to make things a little easier for you."

She studies me for a beat, then glances at the computer again before returning her gaze to mine. "You're so different from who I thought you were when we first met."

I'm not sure what to say, so I say nothing. I can't blame her for thinking one thing when I've tried so hard over the years to appear like the fun-loving guy who doesn't take anything seriously. Maybe I really was him when I was younger, but I haven't been him for some time. For whatever reason, it feels difficult to let people I already know peek behind the curtain to see the real me.

"I had no idea that behind that outward shell you present to the world was such a thoughtful, caring, and considerate man." She kisses the edge of my jaw, then trails her tongue over to my earlobe. "The good-in-bed part I could've guessed." Her hand runs up my thigh and she cups me between my legs.

My half-hard dick twitches under her hand. "I was happy to do it."

"I know. That's what makes it so wonderful." She pulls away from me, and I'm about to protest, but she slides off the couch and sits on her knees between my spread legs. Her fingers manipulate the button on my jeans.

My dick is rock hard between my legs, pushing against my

zipper for escape. "Ash, you don't have to do this just because I created a better website for you."

"What if I want to do this just because?" She gives me a coy grin.

I sink further into the couch. "Well, in that case, have at it."

I spread my arms across the back of the couch and watch as she unzips my fly. When she tugs down my jeans and my underwear, I lift my hips to help her. Once my pants and boxer briefs are around my ankles, she strokes me.

My breath catches in my throat, and I force myself to remember how to breathe as she runs her tongue from the base to the tip. She plays with me for a minute, just sucking on the tip and stroking me. I fist her hair in one hand and hold it above her head so that I can see everything that's happening because I will be beating off to this image in the future.

She strokes me a few times before twirling her tongue around the tip of me, just enough to tease me and set me on edge. My teeth clamp together, wanting to force her down my length, but enjoying her teasing just the same. Ashley finally puts me out of my misery, wrapping her mouth around me and bringing my length to the back of her throat.

My hands tighten in her hair, and I groan as she draws herself back up. She repeats the motion over and over, chasing her mouth with her fist.

God, this woman drives me crazy in the best way.

She works me over, and within minutes, the base of my spine tingles. I stiffen as I breach the back of her throat, and she moans around my cock, the vibrations of the sound echoing down into my balls and drawing them up.

"Ash, I'm close."

Her gaze meets mine, and she doesn't pull away. She pushes her mouth all the way down to my base and holds herself there, moaning. It's all the encouragement I need before my release pours out of me and down the back of her throat. I do my best not to pull her hair too hard, but I'm pretty sure I'm unsuccessful.

Ashley gently sucks until she's drained me, and I fall from her mouth against my thigh. She tilts her head and rests her cheek on my thigh, staring up at me with a small smile as we both calm our breathing.

Gazing down at her, I never want this to end. For the last couple of days, I've been trying to stay in the moment and enjoy our time together, but the ticking of the clock that's running out of time has been getting louder and louder in the background no matter what I do.

After I grow soft, Ashley helps me pull up my boxer briefs and jeans. I zip myself back up and button my jeans. When I'm done, I pull Ashley in, wrapping my arm around her shoulders. She rests her cheek on my chest.

I bask in how right it feels and gather the courage to say what's been on my mind. "Can we talk about the thing we're not talking about?"

She pulls out from under my arm to meet my gaze. "Which is?"

"The fact that I'll be leaving after the wedding."

She swallows hard and moves her gaze toward the fireplace.

"I don't want to leave." If I could somehow extend my stay, I would.

"I know. I don't want you to go either."

I take her hand. "I don't want this to end when I leave."

We haven't talked about what is going on with us, if it's a fling or not, so I can't be sure what she wants to do. It's scary to put myself out there, but I need to know.

"Does that mean you want to try long distance?" Her cheeks pinken, and I know that it was a hard question for her to ask.

"I do, yeah." She opens her mouth to say something, but I cut her off before she can tell me all the reasons long-distance relationships never work. "We're not even that far away from each other. We're in the same time zone, which makes things less complicated. Our states are literally right beside each other."

She shakes her head, a small smile playing on her face. "In the north. Not Manhattan."

"Semantics. I think if we want this to work, we can make it work. I know you don't have the luxury of leaving the B&B unattended, so I'll come visit you. I have all kinds of banked vacation time I've never used. It's just going to take some effort."

"Carter..."

"Please say yes, Ash." I squeeze her hand. I can feel the line between my eyebrows deepening with concern.

"Carter—"

"I don't want this to end."

She brings her hand to my mouth and covers it. "Carter, if you'd let me finish, you'd know that I want to try too."

I pull her in, skirting my tongue on the seam of her lips until she opens for me. Our kiss feels like the sealing of a promise between us.

When I end the kiss, I rest my forehead on hers. "You won't regret this."

"It's going to take a lot of work and effort on both our parts if it's going to work though."

I cup her face and meet her eyes. "I have faith in us."

She smiles, and it's like the warm glow of Christmas lights on my face. "So do I."

Chapter Twenty-One

I wake up to a blanket of snow outside. A very thick, very deep blanket.

Carter has been sleeping in my bed, and when I roll over to look out the window like I do first thing every morning, I'm met with a sheet of falling snow. It should probably be my first indication that things won't go as planned today, but all I see and feel is Carter. I'm in too deep with him, and everything has a rose-colored tint for me.

I'm near the window, looking at the falling snow and how much has already fallen overnight when a set of hands wraps around my waist from behind.

Carter rests his chin on my shoulder. "Good morning."

"Morning." I turn in his arms to face him. "How did you sleep?"

He gives me a cocky grin. Guess he liked how I woke him up in the middle of the night last night. "Much better after our middle-of-the-night activities."

I hum low in my throat. "Same."

"I need to get in the shower and wash up before Steph and

Doug arrive. Thought maybe you could join me. You know, to conserve water."

"Oh, of course, it's all about water conservation."

"I'm nothing if not a staunch environmentalist."

I laugh, burrowing my face into his chest. "Well, if it's to save Mother Earth, then how can I say no?"

Carter pulls away, then bends and throws me over his shoulder, carrying me to the en suite.

I don't bother complaining. There's no point in pretending I don't want to be in his arms.

We take a leisurely shower that involves orgasms—one for him and two for me—then towel off.

"I'm going to go get dressed." Carter kisses the tip of my nose and leaves the en suite.

His clothes are still all in the other room he was staying in. I've thought of telling him to move his things into my room for the rest of his stay, but I wasn't sure if that would seem too forward.

Humming a Christmas carol, I leave the bathroom and choose a sweater and a pair of jeans from my dresser. I've just gotten dressed when my phone rings from where it's plugged in on the nightstand. I walk over and frown, seeing my sister's name on the screen. She should already be up in the air.

"Hello?"

"Where the hell have you been? I've called, like, five times!" My sister's voice is frantic and has that stressed out tone I recognize.

My stomach sinks to the floor like falling snow. "Steph. What's going on? What's wrong?"

"Everything! Everything is wrong!"

I sit on the bed with the phone pressed to my ear. "Why aren't you on a plane?"

"Because there're no flights going into Vermont or the northeast at all."

"What?" My head whips to look out the window, and yeah, the snow is still steadily falling.

"Apparently there's some freak weather event going on. Like, a once-in-a-hundred-years kind of snowstorm."

"Are you serious? I didn't hear anything about that. I mean, I knew it was supposed to snow, and I thought you might get delayed, but that's all."

"I'm not delayed, Ash, I'm not coming. To my own wedding!" She cries and tears automatically form in my own eyes.

I know how much work and money went into this and how much she wants to be married to Doug. I feel horrible for the situation she's in.

"Don't cry, Steph. We're going to figure something out." I rack my brain to keep it together as my sister sobs. I put the phone on speaker and pull up my weather app. "It's supposed to clear out the day before Christmas Eve. Maybe everyone can change their flights and come out then. You could have a Christmas Eve wedding."

"I can't ask everyone to change their holiday plans. Most people were just coming in and out for the wedding. Maybe it's just not meant to be."

My spine stiffens, and I straighten on the edge of the mattress. "You and Doug are meant to be, Steph."

"I know, I know. I mean the wedding. Maybe we should've picked a tropical island to get married on like everyone else. I mean, first I can't make it when I planned to because of work and now this. It just feels like maybe it's not meant to happen the way I envisioned."

I'm quiet for a beat, not sure what to say. I feel devastated for her. "When and how it does happen, it will be magical."

"I feel awful though. You and Carter did so much work for us."

"Don't worry about that. It should be the least of your concerns."

"God, why is this happening to me?"

Tears track down my face as Carter comes back in the room. When he sees the state of me, he stops in his tracks before rushing over and sitting beside me on the bed.

"What do you need me to do?" I ask, trying to pull it together.

"Everyone flying in needs to know the wedding isn't happening," Steph says, and Carter jolts beside me on the bed and widens his eyes. "They probably all assume that, given they can't get there, but I don't want to leave anyone guessing."

"I'll handle it." I sniff and wipe my cheeks with the back of my hand. "I'll call all the vendors too."

"You're the best, Ash." Her voice wobbles, and the sound is a punch to the gut. "I'll call later when I'm calmer."

"You call me whenever. Any time of the day or night, all right?"

"All right, love you."

The line goes dead, and I toss my phone to the side on the mattress.

"What the hell is going on? The wedding's off?" Carter's face is full of confusion, his phone already in his hand, probably ready to call Doug.

I burst into tears, concern for my sister covering me like a blanket. Carter pulls me into his arms and rubs my back, soothing me. Or doing his best to at least.

When I finally compose myself, I pull back and explain the situation to him. He frowns while he listens, forehead wrinkled.

Once I'm done, he blows out a long breath and pushes a hand through his dark hair. "I'm gonna have to call Doug and see how he's doing. I can't believe this."

I nod. "I feel so bad for my sister. You dream of your wedding your whole life and now everything she wanted is ruined."

"What can I do to help?"

More tears track down my cheeks. "I'm too upset to call everyone. I'll probably cry and babble, and no one would understand me. Would you be able to do it if I got you a list with all the names and numbers for the guests? There's not that many since it wasn't a huge wedding to begin with."

"Of course. Whatever you need, I'm here for you. You can count on me."

The words have no sooner left his lips than his phone rings. He fishes it out of his jeans and looks at the screen, appearing annoyed.

"Who is it?" I ask.

"My boss." He lets out a heavy sigh. "I have to answer this." Carter cringes a little and picks up the phone. "Hey."

I listen, crying silent tears as Carter deals with his boss. It's obvious something has gone wrong at work and that he's been tapped in to fix it.

A few minutes after the call begins, Carter says, "Yes, Ralph. I'll make sure it's handled right away."

I'm looking at my hand curled on my lap, but when I hear Carter's comment to his boss, my head whips in his direction.

As he hangs up, he gives me a pleading look. "I'm sorry, I have to take care of this."

This, on top of everything, seems to be the thing that upsets me the most. "You just finished telling me that I can count on you." My despair morphs to anger in my veins.

"You can. I just have to take care of this first. Our biggest client has an issue with the server on their site, and it's right before Christmas. Every minute lost is tens of thousands of dollars for them in lost revenue."

My arms fly up in front of me, almost of their own volition. "By all means then, don't let my personal crisis prevent you from saving the billionaires and the shareholders of the world."

His jaw flexes. "It's not like that. I can't just tell my boss no. As soon as I'm done dealing with this, I'll make those phone calls for you."

"Don't bother. They can't wait." I stand, ready to go down to my office and get the list off my computer.

I move to walk past Carter, but he holds my wrist and stops me from passing him. "Ash, don't be like this. Don't let your temper get the best of you. I'm sorry, okay?"

"This isn't about my temper." I yank my hand from his grip. "I get it. I do. But do you want to know what hurts so much? You're setting me aside for a job you don't even like. One you're not even sure you still want to be doing."

"Regardless, it's still my job currently."

"Aren't you technically on vacation? How am I supposed to feel when you're moving me to the bottom of the list of priorities for something you don't even care that much about? What does that say about how you feel for me?"

He swallows hard. "What? This has nothing to do with how I feel about you."

"Maybe not to you, but to me it does. How are we ever going to make long distance work when you can't even put me first when we're in the same place? How many missed Face-Time calls and canceled trips to see me should I be expecting, Carter? Because this really isn't giving me much confidence, I have to be honest."

He presses his lips together. "You're overreacting."

"Ha!" My chin tilts up as a caustic laugh escapes. "If you want overreacting, I can give that to you." I stomp toward the door, and slam it as hard as I can.

The sound echoes through the hall, and I can't help but think of how final it feels.

Chapter Twenty-Two

CARTER

It takes me two hours to figure out the situation with work. Probably because the entire time, my mind is half on my argument with Ashley. I can't get the hurt look on her face out of my mind.

Knowing I'm the one who put it there doesn't sit well with me. Especially because I know she has a point. I've always been a workaholic, but if I leave this project with my team, Ralph is going to have a field day with me. I need this job until I go out on my own. If I go out on my own.

Ashley is right though. I can't even put her first when I'm on vacation and in the same house as her. How will it work when I'm back in New York and the daily demands of my job are front and center? How can I possibly think that we can successfully do long distance?

I spend the rest of my day in my room, knowing Ashley isn't interested in seeing me, but by the time dinner approaches, I seek her out. But before I leave my bedroom, I make a phone call.

Ashley is in the living room, cuddled up into the corner of

the couch with a holiday quilt over her, watching *Surviving Christmas*.

"Can we talk?"

She doesn't respond or even glance my way.

It's like a slap across the face.

I sigh and sit on the couch, giving her space. "If you tell me you want me to leave, I'll go back upstairs. But I think we should talk about this."

She says nothing, then clicks pause on the movie and shifts to face me. "All right. You have my attention. Talk."

If I were in a better mood, I'd chuckle. This is one way that she's like her sister—stubborn when she's pissed off.

"I'm sorry I let you down. I said I would do something for you, be there for you, and I wasn't." She doesn't respond, but her shoulders relax, and her jaw doesn't appear quite as set, which I take as a good sign, so I continue. "The truth is, you're right. It's going to be hard trying to make this work being so far apart. And if I'm honest, that scares the shit out of me."

Ashley stares at me, then whips the blanket off of her lap onto the floor and crawls toward me. My hands instinctively go to her hips and pull her in so that she's straddling me, her hands on either side of my face.

"I'm scared too. I didn't expect this thing between us, and even if I could have predicted it, I would never have thought it would feel this..."

She searches for the right word, so I say the first one that comes to mind, "All-consuming?"

Ash bites her bottom lip and nods. "That's exactly it."

I close my eyes and rest my forehead against hers. "I'm sorry. I can't promise that I won't fuck up again, I will, but I promise I will always strive to put you first."

She shakes her head. "I overreacted. With the wedding being canceled, my sister in a panic and so distraught, I was already feeling so raw. I was dreading the idea of having to call the whole family and deliver the news about the wedding."

I turn my head and kiss her palm. "I'm sorry I wasn't the one who handled that for you."

"No, it was good actually. Talking to my parents and my aunts and everyone else helped me feel a little better about the situation. They put my mind at ease that it would still happen, just not how they originally planned."

"Steph and Doug love each other. No way they're letting this stop them from spending the rest of their lives together."

She nods. "Yeah. It's still disappointing, but I truly do believe that everything happens for a reason."

"So... you forgive me then?" I arch an eyebrow.

Ash gives me a small smile and nods. The mood between us is still somber, so I attempt to lighten it.

"Does this mean we get to have our first makeup sex now?"

Her head rocks back in laughter. I lean forward, dragging my tongue from the base of her throat up to her ear. It elicits a moan from her.

"First of firsts?" she whispers.

"Exactly. I want this to work so badly, Ash."

She tips her head down and brings her lips to mine. The kiss starts off slow and sensual but quickly morphs to heated and full of desire. Soon we're tugging off each other's clothes, tossing them wherever they fall, and then she's over me, sliding down my length until I'm fully seated inside her. We both take a moment to enjoy the sensation of having her wrapped around me, neither of us moving as we breathe in each other's air.

She moves on top of me. I take her nipple in my mouth, sucking gently and nibbling on the hard peak. Her hands dive into my hair, and she pulls, mixing pain with the pleasure.

Within minutes, we're both panting after our releases and

catching our breath. She's locked in my arms, pressed against my chest with my face buried in her neck. I'm completely satisfied, yet a feeling of panic, unrivaled from any other time in my life, rises as though it might swallow me whole.

I can't lose this. I can't lose her. I can't.

But am I destined to lose her if I return to New York and pick up where I left off on my life there?

I sit with that thought, breathing in her scent. The answer is yes. If I try to continue this so far away from her, I most definitely will lose her, and that is not an option.

An idea forms.

I've done some crazy shit in my life, but somehow, what I'm picturing isn't one of them.

Chapter Twenty-Three

ASHLEY

Carter and I spend the day after our fight in my bed while the snowstorm creates havoc for the rest of the area.

It must have stopped some time overnight because when I roll over and look out the window, it's clear out. Mistletoe Falls is used to snowstorms, so the roads will be cleared by lunch, and everyone will go about their business as though the blizzard never happened.

Today would have been my sister's wedding. I mentally note to call her and see how she's doing, though I suspect better than most since yesterday evening she sent me links to tropical resorts, asking me which one would be better for her wedding.

I roll over to Carter's side of the bed to see if he's awake, but it's empty. I sit up, holding the sheet to my naked chest and looking around the room, listening for the shower. This is the first morning he hasn't been in bed when I've woken. My hand falls to his pillow and lands on a piece of paper.

Ash,

Have a few things to do. Probably won't be home until late afternoon. See you then.
- C

What does this cryptic message mean? What does he have to do? Carter is supposed to leave the day after tomorrow to fly to Oregon and spend the holidays with his family. I wanted to spend as much time with him as I could since I don't have any guests arriving until after New Year's. I'm all caught up in my feelings until I wonder why he's going to be gone majority of the day.

What could he possibly be doing?

I slump back in bed. What am I going to do with my day now? Then it dawns on me that for the first time in years, I won't be spending my holidays catering to guests and making sure they're taken care of. Sure, Christmas Eve and Christmas Day will probably feel a little lonely, but I'll be sure to Face-Time my sister and my parents, and Carter.

Excited about the possibilities, I bound out of bed for the shower. Once I've showered and dressed, I head to the basement to get a box of Christmas crafts I bought years ago, intending to make them but never having the time.

Rather than picking through the box in the unfinished basement, I bring the box upstairs into the great room. I set up another one of my favorite Christmas movies, *Four Christmases*, and go to the kitchen to make hot chocolate.

By late afternoon, I've turned the movies off and have Christmas carols ringing through my speakers. I'm singing along as I try my best to get the hang of the embroidery, attempting an ornament.

I'm feeling light as air, singing at the top of my lungs. I spoke with my sister earlier and she seems to be more interested in moving forward with new wedding plans than dwelling on the failed one. I have some unexpected time on my hands to do what I want, and I've unexpectedly fallen head over heels for a new man.

When the song comes to an end, clapping rings out, and I look to my right. Carter's leaning against the doorframe, smiling wide.

"I didn't hear you come in."

My stomach flutters like a thousand little snowflakes falling to the ground because Carter looks good. He's wearing a pair of jeans that fit him perfectly and a blue sweater that makes his eyes pop. But more than that, it's the way he's looking at me, as if maybe he feels the same way about me as I do for him.

"I know." He pushes off the doorframe and steps into the room. "I wasn't about to interrupt such a wonderful performance."

I roll my eyes.

"Are you hungry? I come bearing gifts," he says, and I tilt my head. "Wait here. I took it into the kitchen so I could grab some cutlery."

When he leaves, I turn the music down to a conversational level and tidy up all the embroidery floss and needle. He returns holding a large paper bag in one hand, cutlery in the other.

"What's this?"

"I called your favorite restaurant in town on my way back." He sets the bag and the cutlery on the coffee table.

"You know my favorite restaurant?"

He shrugs. "You told me about it on our date in New York, and I committed the name to memory. Remember you were comparing the burrata there to the one you order from the place here?"

I didn't remember, but now I do. I can't believe he

remembers that, especially after the way that night ended. "That's so sweet of you, Carter, thanks."

"I didn't want you to have to cook tonight." Before I can ask why, he's taking everything out of the bags. "I also got some Caesar salad as an appetizer and a few pasta dishes since I wasn't sure which one you liked. The owner said you order a few off the menu when you're there."

My chest warms, and my smile grows. "You talked to Andy? I'm speechless. Thank you."

"You being speechless tells me that all the other men you've had in your life haven't treated you right. I'm going to show you what you're worth." He sits on the couch beside me, and with his thumb and forefinger on my chin, he pulls me in for a kiss.

I sink into his touch, feeling with my whole body how much I missed him today.

When he finally pulls away before things get too out of hand, he says, "Let's eat."

We decide to both have a little of everything, and by the time we're done eating, I can't imagine eating another bite.

"That was delicious."

Carter hums his agreement. "I can see why you love this place." He gets up from the couch, and I go to do the same, but he gently sets his hand on my shoulder. "You relax. I'll clean up."

"I can help."

"I know you can. But you're always waiting on other people. Let me for once." He kisses the end of my nose before collecting the cutlery and containers and leaving the room.

While he's gone, I turn off the music system, assuming he'll want to watch TV or something. I can't believe how far I've fallen and how fast. It seems insane to think that just a short time ago, I thought of him as the world's biggest jerk, but now... now the thought of him leaving makes me feel physically ill.

"What's wrong?"

Carter's voice startles me, and I watch him walk toward me. There's no reason to pretend nothing is wrong. If we're going to have a successful long-distance relationship, good communication is key.

"I was just thinking about how you have to leave soon." I frown. "I know we're going to keep seeing each other, but I'm going to miss having you here."

He draws in a deep breath, and if I didn't know better, I'd say he looks nervous. "I'm so glad to hear you say that." He closes the distance, setting his hands on my hips, pulling me in. "I feel the same way. I don't want this to end, and last night I thought, maybe it doesn't have to."

My forehead wrinkles. I'm not sure what he's talking about, but I assume it has something to do with the reason he was gone most of the day. When I asked him while we were eating what he was up to today, he told me I would find out later. At the time I thought maybe he was out looking for a Christmas present for me, but now I'm not so sure.

"What do you mean?" I ask.

"What I'm about to say is going to sound insane, but all I ask is that you hear me out, all right?"

"Okay..."

Carter cups my face. "Ashley, we had a connection the moment we met, and yes, when I say the moment, I mean New York. I know I freaked out and everything, but it wasn't because I didn't feel an immediate draw to you. I just thought it was because of my long-standing friendship with your sister. But it didn't take long for me to figure out after coming here that the connection I felt was all because of you. You are the most thoughtful, caring, and selfless woman I've known, and you're gorgeous on top of it. You're sexy, but at the same time you have no idea just how much. I love how you embarrass so easily and the way your cheeks get pink. I love how you care about your community and your neighbors and always strive to do your best no matter what the task is. There's so much I already know about you, but there's also so much more I want to discover." He swallows and releases a shuddering breath. "I know you don't think of yourself as a spontaneous person, but I would disagree. You bought this B&B in a different state, away from everything and everyone you've ever known, and took a chance that it would work out. What I'm asking you now is to take another big chance—on us."

He drops onto one knee, and all the air leaves my lungs in a whoosh. He pulls a gorgeous antique art déco ring from his pocket, and I gasp. I know exactly where it's from—the jewelry store in town. It's been in their window for months, and every time I walk by, I admire it.

"Ashley, I love you, and I don't want this to end. Ever. I know it's fast, and I know people will have their opinions, but I already know I want to spend the rest of my life with you. I don't need to spend another year enduring a long-distance relationship to know you're *it* for me. You're my person. Will you marry me?"

My stomach swoops as if I'm charging down the track of a roller coaster in the last car. "But you live in New York."

I don't know why that's the first thing out of my mouth and not immediately the word no. But it's the first thing that pops in my head, that we can't be married and live in different states.

He shakes his head. "I'm quitting my job. Starting my own business like I've wanted to for years, the same way you did when you bought this place. I can do that job from anywhere, so I can stay in Mistletoe Falls, with you."

Excitement bubbles in my stomach and fizzles in my veins. Am I really considering this?

God, yes. Yes, I am.

Since the moment I met Carter, something just felt right about him. Solid. As though he'd finally taken his place in my life as he was always meant to. Maybe that's why I was so upset after our first date when he rejected me outright. I questioned how I could be so wrong about the connection between us.

Carter doesn't pressure me for an answer while I stand silent. He just looks up at me with a hopeful expression on his face while I work it out in my head.

But it doesn't take me long to know my answer. "Yes! Yes, I'll marry you."

Tears fill my eyes as he slides the ring onto my finger. It's a perfect fit as if he measured my ring finger. He stands and takes my face in his hands, pulling me in for a kiss. We both laugh and cry happy tears while our lips mingle together. It's much too short when he abruptly pulls away.

"What's wrong?" I ask.

He cringes. "I practiced my speech all day in my head, and I can't believe I missed the second most important part."

"What?"

"I want us to get married tonight."

My mouth drops open. "Tonight?"

"Today was supposed to be Steph and Doug's day, so everything is already in motion for there to be a wedding this evening. I want it to be ours. I don't want to waste any time starting my life with you."

His request is the single most romantic thing I've heard in my life. Maybe a little insane, but romantic, nonetheless.

It doesn't take me more than half a second to think about it before I blurt, "Yes!"

We crash together in another kiss, and when we pull away this time, he rests his forehead on mine, his hands holding my face to his.

"Are we crazy for doing this?" I ask.

"Probably, but it doesn't make it wrong."

"It doesn't feel wrong."

He smiles at me. "No, it doesn't."

"What am I going to wear? It's not like I have a wedding dress lying around."

He arches an eyebrow. "Actually, you do."

"There's no way I'm wearing my sister's wedding dress."

He laughs. "Wear your bridesmaid's dress then. You'll look beautiful in whatever you wear, Ash. I just want to marry you." He runs a hand down my arm.

"That's actually a good idea. I'll wear the bridesmaid's dress, and you can wear the suit you have for the wedding."

"Perfect. You don't have to do anything other than get yourself ready. I have a couple calls to make now that you've said yes, so meet me at the altar in three hours."

I nod. "In three hours, you'll be my husband."

He smiles, and it feels like the warmth of sunshine on my face after a long winter. "I promise you won't regret this."

Chapter Twenty-Four

CARTER

Three hours later, I wait with the officiant in the room that Steph and Doug were meant to get married in.

I still can't believe she said yes.

It's odd, but no part of me is nervous about what I'm about to do. I'm only excited and ready to make Ashley my wife.

The hairdresser Ashley uses in town was here earlier to do her hair, as was a makeup artist. The chairs we picked up are lined up, even though there are no guests. Vermont doesn't require witnesses to the marriage, and Ashley and I decided that if our loved ones couldn't be present today, it would just be the two of us.

Maybe we'll have some sort of celebration down the road and include all our friends and family. Maybe not. All I care about is officially making Ashley mine.

Both Ash and I decided not to tell our families yet though. Neither of us is interested in hearing their opinions, and let's face it, they'd try to talk us out of it. There's no possible way they'd understand the connection we have. It's something they'll have to see for themselves to believe. If they don't like it after, then so be it.

Classic renditions of Christmas carols play in the background. Anna brought our dinner over earlier and left it in the oven to stay warm. She was even gracious enough to bake a small wedding cake for us this afternoon after we spoke.

I'm deep in thought, running through everything, double-checking we're all set when Ashley appears at the end of the aisle.

Jesus, this woman takes my breath away. Her hair is curled, half up, half down. She has a little more makeup than usual, and it makes her look sexy while still maintaining her innocent vibe. Her deep green, off-the-shoulder dress brings out the red in her hair. She holds a small bouquet with red amaryllis and Christmas roses.

I never believed in that whole theory about taking a person's breath away, but looking at her and knowing she's agreed to marry me steals all oxygen in the room. Her smile when she sees me only flames that feeling more. It's as if all the joy and happiness inside me expands my chest, leaving little room for air.

She walks down the aisle, and I thank the powers that be for giving me another chance with this woman. Someone or something was on my side for me to be here right now.

She stops at the end of the aisle, glancing at the decor, the officiant, everything I did while she's been getting ready. "Carter, how did you pull this off?"

"Ester helped. Then Anna called in some favors with the county clerk, and lucky for us, her father is a judge." I nod toward the officiant, and he dips his head toward Ashley in greeting.

"I can't believe we're getting married." Her eyes water.

"Me either. But it feels right, doesn't it?"

She nods. "Absolutely."

"Shall we begin?" the judge asks.

We smile one last time at one another before facing him and nodding.

"Dearly beloved..." He pauses. "I guess we can skip that part."

The three of us laugh.

"We're gathered here today to unite this man and this woman in holy matrimony." He continues with all the usual ceremony lingo, then we get to the vows and the exchange of rings. "I understand that you've both prepared your own vows?"

Ashley and I nod, keeping our eyes on one another.

"All right, Carter, you start."

I squeeze Ashley's hands. "Ash, I love you. Not just in the easy, effortless way that love sometimes begins, but in a deep, steady way. I know without a doubt that my love for you will only grow stronger with every year we face together. Thank you for trusting me enough to stand beside me today. That trust you give me is the greatest honor of my life. I want you to know that I don't take your happiness lightly. From this day forward, it becomes my purpose. Your joy, your safety, your peace of mind are my sacred responsibilities. I promise to protect the beautiful life we build together, to keep it full of laughter, warmth, and unshakable love. I promise to be the man you can count on, even when I fall short because let's face it, I will. But I will own it, I will listen, and I will grow. I promise to be faithful not only in body, but in heart and mind. I promise to love you without conditions, nor hesitation. I promise to stand by you in the hard times and dance with you in the good. Mostly, I promise to choose us—again and again, every single day."

Tears fill her eyes as I finish. Her smile is so wide it makes me believe that she enjoyed my vows.

The officiant turns to my fiancée. Man, I wasn't able to use that word for long. "Your turn, Ashley."

"Carter, standing here with you today might be the most impulsive thing I've ever done—and yet, it's also the most certain I've ever felt. So maybe it isn't impulsive at all. Maybe it's fate. From the moment we met, there was this inexplicable pull—like something in the universe whispered to me. When you were brought back into my life, it wasn't a coincidence. It was serendipity. Working side by side, watching you laugh, learning the way your mind works and the way your heart gives, a quiet certainty rose inside me. A belief that maybe we were always meant to find our way back to each other. Do you remember the holiday dance? When we each wrote a wish and hung it on the tree? I wished that if you and I were truly meant to be, I wouldn't have to question it. That the universe would give me a sign. And then you came on one knee, asking me to choose forever with you. That was my sign. That was the moment I stopped wondering and simply knew. We were always meant to find each other again. And this—us—feels like home."

I can't believe we both wished something about the other that night.

"I vow to love you and support you, to be the person you can tell anything to without fear of judgment and to always be in your corner. I too will put us first, and I promise to always remember the feeling that brought us here today and work to preserve it."

A single tear slips down her cheek, and I brush it away with my thumb.

"Do you have rings to exchange?" the officiant asks.

I reach into the inside pocket of my suit jacket and pull out both rings, handing the wedding band meant for me to Ashley.

We recite the more traditional vows as we each slide a ring on each other's finger.

"With the power vested in me, I now pronounce you husband and wife. You may kiss your bride."

I waste no time, pulling Ashley into me and kissing her thoroughly. It's only when the officiant clears his throat that we separate.

"I just need you two to sign, then I'm out of here." He leads us to the small table that Steph and Doug were supposed to sign at, and once we've both signed on the dotted line, he looks at us with a big smile. "I wish you both a lifetime of happiness together. Congratulations."

We say thank you, and once he's gone, it's just the two of us. Ashley and I look at each other and burst out laughing.

"I can't believe we're married." She covers her mouth and laughs again.

"We're officially husband and wife." My smile will never fade knowing she's my wife. "Care to have our first dance now?" I place my hands on her hips and pull her toward me.

"Absolutely."

I pull my phone from my pocket that's hooked up to the Bluetooth speaker and play the song I picked out for our first dance—mostly because I know Ash loves it, but also because we can slow dance to it.

Frank Sinatra's "Have Yourself a Merry Little Christmas" plays, and I increase the volume before dropping my phone on the table and pulling my wife close. She rests her check on my chest, and I secure her in my arms.

"You know my wish was about you too?" I admit a minute or so later.

She lifts her head and looks up at me. "It was?"

I nod. "When I was trying to figure out what to wish for, I tried to clear my mind so that whatever was most important would pop to the surface. The vision that arose was of you wearing a wedding dress. I wished for my vision to come true."

Ash frowns and looks down between us. "But I'm not wearing a wedding dress."

"Ah, but you were. The day I barged in on you at the seamstress's, you were. And it was exactly what I saw in my mind that night. I knew then that we'd eventually make it here."

"I don't care what anyone says when they find out we're married, I know we're meant to be."

I bend my head and kiss her, slow and thorough. The tension between us builds until we're both breathing hard when we pull away from each other.

"Speaking of our friends and family finding out, I have something to ask you," I say.

"I already agreed to marry you today. You're pushing your luck." She giggles.

"Will you come with me to Oregon for the holidays? You don't have any guests, and I want you to meet my family. But if you don't want to or can't for whatever reason, then I'll stay here with you. No matter what, we're spending Christmas together."

Her fingers run through the hair at the back of my head. "I would love to join you. I can't wait to meet the family I've just married into."

I kiss her again, but this time when I pull away, I don't say anything. I lead her upstairs by the hand to the bedroom to make love to my wife.

Dinner can wait.

Chapter Twenty-Five

CARTER

"Wait." Ashley reaches for my wrist and stops me before I open the car door of our rental. "I'm nervous. What if they don't like me?"

I remove my hand from the door handle and shift to face her. Taking her hand, I run my thumb over her wedding ring, as I've done numerous times since I slid it on there. "There's nothing to be concerned about. They're going to love you."

She dips her chin and gives me a look. "They don't even know I exist, let alone that we're married. I really think you should have called and told them before we arrived."

"It will be fine, I promise. Sure, they'll be surprised, but I promise you that once the shock wears off, they're going to welcome you with open arms."

I'm going to make sure they're open-minded and understand that this isn't one of my impulsive decisions... well, maybe it is. But it's not the *wrong* decision.

I place a chaste kiss on her lips then exit the vehicle. I leave all our bags inside, too eager for my family to meet the woman I love.

Ash grips my hand tightly as we walk up the path toward my childhood home.

Once we're outside the front door, I spin around to face her. "There's one more thing you should know."

Her head tilts. "What?"

"My brother's wife and I dated briefly before she met him randomly and ended up marrying him. It's not a big deal, and it's not weird between us or anything, but in case it comes up in conversation or something, I don't want you to be surprised. I'd never want you to think I was keeping secrets."

"Okay, you couldn't have told me on the plane at least?"

"I just never think about it. You're not upset, are you?"

The look on her face says she's not so sure about it, but she shakes her head. "No."

I place a quick kiss on her lips before turning to face the door again. I open the door. Ash drops my hand and hangs behind me as I step inside.

"Hello?" I shout.

"In here," my mom calls from the kitchen.

My stomach flips as I lead Ashley to the back of the house. I can't remember the last time I was this nervous. Actually, only a couple days ago when I asked Ashley to marry me and I wasn't sure if she'd say yes. I just want everyone to accept her with open arms, and I want her to love my family since they're such a big part of my life.

"Ryah, where are you?" I ask, stepping into the room, excited to have my niece run into my arms.

"Yeah, no go, big brother. She's stuck to Pierce like he's gingerbread frosting," Brynn says.

I don't know what she's talking about, I'm Ryah's favorite. "Maybe for you, but not for me." I hold out my arms for my niece—who completely ignores my existence. I can't say it doesn't hurt a little.

That's when everyone notices Ashley standing behind me.

"Oh hi," Tessa says, wiping her hands on her apron. "I'm Tessa."

"Oh, sorry, guys, this is Ashley. My wife." I can't hold in my grin. It just feels so good to call her my wife.

Ashley lifts her hand, and her ring sparkles under the kitchen lights. "Hi." She's putting up a good front, but her voice is a little shaky.

"What?" everyone says in unison.

Huh. Maybe I should've taken Ashley's advice and given them the heads-up.

They all stare at us in disbelief, shock written all over their faces.

"Yeah, what?" Dad walks in from the other room, his shirt dirty from chopping wood for the fireplace.

"I got married." I'm probably beaming like a teenage girl at her first Taylor Swift concert, but I don't care. They need to see how happy I am. They need to get behind this and us.

"We got that part, Carter," Dad says. I can't tell from his voice whether he's displeased or not.

"Sorry, remember when I went to that destination wedding? Well, Ashley was a bridesmaid, and I was a grooms-man, and we just kind of hit it off."

"And got married?" Brynn asks, eyeing Pierce and Tre. Their expressions are the same as hers, pure shock.

"I know this is weird. I told him to tell you before we arrived." Ashley hides behind me, resting her forehead on my shoulder.

"Well, Carter's weird, so get used to it." Brynn pulls some dough out of the bowl in front of her and pops it into her mouth. When she reaches for another, Tre slaps her hand.

I decide to ignore their shock and skepticism. They'll figure out soon enough that Ashley and I are the real thing. I look back at my niece. "Ryah, seriously? I want to introduce you to your new aunt."

She looks up but doesn't say anything.

"Nice try, but unless Ashley has an English accent, you're wasting your time," Brynn says.

"Are you suggesting she only wants me because of my accent?" her boyfriend, Pierce, asks.

"Well, it's why *I* wanted you." She gives him a cheeky smile.

"It's okay, Pierce, throw it at her." Tre offers him a cinnamon candy.

Brynn opens her mouth, and Pierce tosses it in like a good boyfriend.

Shock and skepticism I expected, but ignoring Ashley isn't an option. "Hello? I just announced I'm married," I say with my hands out at my sides.

Everyone scrambles to their feet and rushes us.

"Sorry, Ashley," Mom says, handing my niece Maisie off to Brynn. "It can get a little crazy around here."

"It's fine," Ashley says, allowing my mom and dad to officially congratulate her and welcome her to the family.

Soon she's at the table with all of us, making sugar cookies, and when I ask her to join me upstairs for a nap, she declines. I can admit to pouting a bit, but Ash kisses my cheek and whispers in my ear that she'll make it up to me tonight. She wants to stay and get to know my family better.

* * *

Later that night, my parents and the littles are asleep. It's just us siblings and our partners hanging out around the dining room table, playing a card game while Christmas carols play in the background.

"You guys are sure there's no booze in this eggnog, right?" I glance at Ash at my side and squeeze her thigh.

She smiles at me.

"For the tenth time, there's no booze in it. What's with the eggnog interrogation?" Brynn asks.

"The two of us went to the holiday dance in my small town," Ash says. "We drank eggnog all night thinking there was no alcohol in it, but there was a mix-up, and we ended up pretty drunk."

"You ended up pretty drunk," I say, then laugh.

She rolls her eyes. "I wasn't the one up on stage for the Santa Strip Tease."

"Gross." Brynn's face screws up as she looks across the table and plays her card.

"I gotta hear about this," Tre says.

"I can do better than that. Someone there sent me a video." Ash pulls her phone out of her back pocket.

My new wife proceeds to show my family the video of me doing a pseudo strip tease.

"You look really happy," my brother says.

"I am." I wrap my arm around Ash's shoulders and pull her into my side, kissing her temple.

"That must be so cool owning a B&B," Tessa says. "Tre and I stayed at one once." She eyes my brother, and they share that look that I never understood. Until now.

"I hope you know when she says that, it means she one hundred percent has plans to come visit and stay there." Tre kisses Tessa's cheek and whispers something in her ear about nutcrackers. Tessa blushes.

"I'd love to have you all at the B&B. We'd have a lot of fun." Ashley sips her drink and looks at the cards in her hand, deciding what to play.

Things were a little awkward at the start, but as the hours ticked by, she became more and more comfortable with my family, and now she's settled right in.

"We should spend next Christmas there," Brynn says.

"Way to invite yourself," Tre says.

Brynn throws a cheeseball at him, and it pings off his forehead. "I meant if she wasn't already booked."

Ash shakes her head. "I only open the dates a year ahead of time, so I can block them off." She knocks me with her shoulder. "Well, my expert IT husband can do it for me."

I love the idea of my family coming out to Vermont to visit us next year. So much so that I pull my phone from my back pocket, log into the backend of Ashley's website, and block off the dates. "Done."

"I've never been to Vermont. Looking forward to it. You have ski slopes, right?" Pierce says in his posh English accent, glancing at Brynn. The two of them and their need to compete on what's better, skis or snowboarding. I love Pierce, and I hate to side with my sister, but snowboarding is so much better.

"What did your family say when you told them you got married, Ashley?" Brynn glances at me as though she's worried.

"My parents were pissed. My mom specifically. But I honestly think a big part of it is that she didn't get to attend the wedding, or more accurately, she didn't get to plan a big wedding. My sister hired a wedding planner, so she missed out with her as well. We FaceTimed my sister and Doug, and that went surprisingly well. They were shocked, of course, because as far as they knew, I didn't like Carter."

"Not surprising. What boneheaded thing did my brother do to make you hate him?" Brynn asks.

"You don't want to know, sis, trust me," I say, and Ash and I share a chuckle.

"Doug and Steph were happy for us, but also a little upset that they missed the wedding. But they're excited because now when we see each other, it'll be a lot of fun since I'm coupled up with their best friend."

"I think it's romantic," Tessa says with a sigh, setting her chin on her hand. "Falling in love at Christmas is the most magical time."

Tre kisses her cheek.

Pierce kisses Brynn's cheek.

I kiss Ashley's cheek.

All three of the Russell kids fell in love at Christmastime. Who could ever have predicted that?

"Agreed. I never could have guessed we'd end up here, but there really are Christmas miracles," I say.

"God, love has made you sappy." Brynn tosses a piece of the cookie at me, and I shift, opening my mouth wide and catching it.

After I finish chewing, I look at my wife. "If sappy feels this good, I'll take it."

ASHLEY

There's a knock at the bedroom door, but before I answer it, I look at my reflection in the mirror.

I think back to last year at this time and how I was getting married. This year, Carter and I are headed to the same hall the holiday dance was at to celebrate our union. So many people in our lives regretted not being able to celebrate with us on our big day, so we decided to have a reception while Carter's family is in town for the holidays.

It seems like the perfect way to share our joy with everyone who means the most to us.

Once I fix my hair a little, check my makeup, I take a deep breath.

The plan is that everyone else is already at the hall, and Carter and I will arrive after. The DJ will announce us like he would at a regular reception, then we'll enjoy a night of drinks and dancing with all our favorite people. Carter's whole family will be there. My parents, Steph, and Doug flew in with some other members of our family, and some of our friends from town will be there as well.

True to his word, Carter quit his job as soon as he

returned to the office after the holidays last year and moved to Mistletoe Falls. The past year has been magical, as if the holidays never ended. We've carried the feeling throughout the whole year.

My hand wraps around the door handle, and I swing open the door. Carter's there, as I knew he would be, and for not the first time this year, he seems speechless.

I didn't tell him I would be wearing a wedding dress. I just said that I was going to wear a fancy dress, and I wanted it to be a surprise until we were ready to leave for the party.

"I wanted to make your vision come true, but with my own wedding gown."

His gaze trails over my body from head to toe and back up.

"Say something." I shift my weight, feeling a little self-conscious.

And he still doesn't. Not even when he steps into the room, placing his hands on my cheeks, and kisses me. He deepens the kiss, and a low groan erupts from his chest.

When he ends the kiss, he rests his forehead on mine. "You look like a dream. Like my vision. How the hell did I get so lucky?"

I smile and run my hand down his strong back. "I'm glad you like it."

He pulls back, holding my hands and pulling them out to the side. "I love it, Ash. But I feel kind of bad because I'm having some really dirty thoughts about what I want to do to you in this dress later tonight."

I laugh. "I was counting on it." Wrapping my arms around his neck, I draw him close. "Are you ready to do this?"

"Celebrate the fact that I somehow convinced you to marry me? Hell yes."

We give each other a quick kiss and make our way down to the front door and out to the truck. Carter drives, and when we reach the hall, we take a moment before getting out of the truck and stepping into the cold.

He takes my hand. "I know I've said this before, Ash, but you're the best thing to ever come into my life. Thank you for giving me another chance, for giving us a chance."

"Carter, I should be the one thanking you. If you hadn't taken a leap of faith and asked me to marry you, who knows where we'd be today."

Carter's new consulting business is going well. He's not making what he was at his fancy tech job in Manhattan, but the business has been growing every month. It's more than enough for us to enjoy a comfortable life in Mistletoe Falls.

"Let's go have fun." He hurries around to the other side of the truck and opens the door for me, helping me down onto the pavement. After taking one look at my shoes, he picks me up and carries me toward the doors. "I don't want you to ruin your shoes or this dress. Maybe our daughter can wear it one day."

We haven't talked about having kids yet, but I've daydreamed about it more and more. When our eyes meet, I'm pretty sure it's the same for Carter.

"Let's do this so we can get home to bed faster." He kisses me before opening the door and setting me down on my feet.

Carter pulls his phone out to text the DJ and let him know that we've arrived, as planned, and a minute later, we're striding through the doors into the hall to the cheers of all our friends and family. After we've made the rounds and said our hellos to everyone, we have our first dance—again. We don't change our song, dancing to Frank Sinatra, and just like when we were here last year, rather than drinking wine or champagne, Carter and I have spiked eggnog.

"No stripping tonight though, okay?" I smile.

"Not even later, when we're alone?" He arches an eyebrow.

"Well… of course then."

He kisses the tip of my nose. I love it when he does that.

I'm tackled in a bear hug from behind by my sister, while Carter and Doug do the man hug thing.

My sister and Doug were married in St. Lucia a couple of months ago, and it was perfect, as we all hoped it would be.

"I still can't believe you're my brother-in-law," Steph says to Carter, giving him a hug.

Doug kisses my cheek.

"Yup, you're really stuck with me now." Carter laughs.

"Wouldn't have it any other way," Steph says, obviously meaning it.

"Where's Mom and Dad?" I ask, looking around.

Steph rolls her eyes. "Talking to your parents, Carter, about all the reasons they should move to Florida once they retire."

"She's obsessed," I say to my sister.

"You should have heard how many times Mom complained that she's freezing in the frigid north tonight before you guys came. You'd think she's in a bikini lying in the snow."

Brynn comes over and whispers something into Carter's ear, and his gaze flicks over to me.

"I'll be right back. There's something I need to do," he says.

I want to ask where he's going, but he doesn't give me the chance, rushing off with his sister.

"What was that about?" Steph asks.

"I have no idea." I shrug.

Doug shakes his head. "Did you see the gleam in his eye? It can only mean bad things."

The three of us laugh, but honestly, Doug is probably right.

A few minutes later, Carter, holding a big red box with a

sparkly green bow on it, heads across the room toward the stage. He says something to the DJ, who lowers the volume on the music and hands a microphone to Carter.

"Hey, everyone, sorry to interrupt the fun, but I wanted to take a moment to thank you all for coming. Both Ash and I appreciate you making the time to celebrate with us, especially during such a busy time of the year."

I make my way toward the stage. We'd planned on saying a few words to welcome everyone and thank them for celebrating with us, but I'd assumed Carter would give me the heads-up beforehand.

"The moment I met Ash, I knew we shared a connection, but what I couldn't have predicted or planned on was how much our connection would grow with every day we're together. I always loved this time of year, but even more so now. The holidays will forever remind me of falling in love with you, Ash, and because of that, it will always be my favorite time of year because you're my favorite person."

Everyone in the hall *awws* as tears spring to my eyes.

"I'm proud to call you my wife, and I wouldn't change a thing about our story because it's led us here. I just wanted to take a moment to give you a very much belated wedding gift. Can you come up onstage?"

My hand goes to my stomach. I had no idea he had planned to get me a wedding gift. But that's my husband—impulsive and forever a romantic.

When I get to the stairs, Carter helps me up. Once I'm standing on the stage with him, he gestures to the box. "Go ahead and open it."

The box rests on the end of the DJ table. I have no idea what it could be, but I walk over and lift the lid. It drops from my hands, and I cover my mouth as I gasp.

"What is it?" someone in the crowd calls.

Nestled on a blanket inside the box is a puppy—a dachshund.

"A puppy," I tell them.

I'd mentioned to Carter a few months ago that I always wanted one growing up but that my mom was allergic to dogs. I don't know why I'm surprised Carter remembered. He always does.

Arms wrap around me from behind, circling my waist. "Do you like your present?"

I nod. "I love it, thank you. She's so sweet. She? He?"

He chuckles in my ear. "She."

"She's so sweet. I almost hate to pick her up and wake her."

"I thought maybe we could practice being fur parents with her before we try for the real thing."

I whip around to face him. "You want to start a family?"

He nods. "I want to start a family with you. But only if you're ready."

A laugh bubbles out of me. "Since when have we waited until we're ready to do anything?"

"Such a wise woman." He kisses me, and the guests clap and cheer.

"We should probably get started tonight. It could take a while." I grin at him.

"Like I said, you're a wise woman."

We kiss again, then we spend the night dancing and celebrating with everyone. And this time when we write down our wishes to add to the tree, I know that the wish of our hearts is about adding to our family.

And twelve months later, we do.

The End

Also by Piper Rayne

Holiday Romances

Single and Ready to Jingle

Claus and Effect

Merry Kissmas

Yule Be Mine

The Nest

Mr. Heartbreaker

Mr. Broody

Mr. Swoony

Mr. Charming

Hockey Hotties

Countdown to a Kiss

My Lucky #13

The Trouble with #9

Faking it with #41

Tropical Hat Trick (Novella)

Sneaking around with #34

Second Shot with #76

Offside with #55

Chicago Grizzlies

On the Defense

Something like Hate

Something like Lust

Something like Love

Kingsmen Football Stars

False Start

You Had Your Chance, Lee Burrows

You Can't Kiss the Nanny, Brady Banks

Over My Brother's Dead Body, Chase Andrews

Modern Love

Charmed by the Bartender

Hooked by the Boxer

Mad about the Banker

Single Dads Club

Real Deal

Dirty Talker

Sexy Beast

Hollywood Hearts

Mister Mom

Animal Attraction

Domestic Bliss

Bedroom Games

Cold as Ice

On Thin Ice

Break the Ice

Chicago Law

Smitten with the Best Man

Tempted by my Ex-Husband

Seduced by my Ex's Divorce Attorney

Blue Collar Brothers

Flirting with Fire

Crushing on the Cop

Engaged to the EMT

White Collar Brothers

Sexy Filthy Boss

Dirty Flirty Enemy

Wild Steamy Hook-up

The Rooftop Crew

My Bestie's Ex

A Royal Mistake

The Rival Roomies

Our Star-Crossed Kiss

The Do-Over

A Co-Workers Crush

The Baileys

Lessons from a One-Night Stand

Advice from a Jilted Bride

Birth of a Baby Daddy

Operation Bailey Wedding (Novella)

Falling for My Brother's Best Friend

Demise of a Self-Centered Playboy

Confessions of a Naughty Nanny

Operation Bailey Babies (Novella)

Secrets of the World's Worst Matchmaker

Winning my Best Friend's Girl

Rules for Dating Your Ex

Operation Bailey Birthday (Novella)

The Greene Family

My Twist of Fortune

My Beautiful Neighbor

My Almost Ex

My Vegas Groom

A Greene Family Summer Bash (Novella)

My Sister's Flirty Friend

My Unexpected Surprise

My Famous Frenemy

A Greene Family Vacation (Novella)

My Scorned Best Friend

My Fake Fiancé

My Brother's Forbidden Friend

A Greene Family Christmas (Novella)

Lake Starlight

The Problem with Second Chances

The Issue with Bad Boy Roommates

The Trouble with Runaway Brides

The Drawback of Single Dads

The Complication with the Best Man

Plain Daisy Ranch

One Last Summer

The One I Left Behind

The One I Stood Beside

The One I Didn't See Coming

Chasing Forever

Chasing Love

Chasing Home

Love in Apartment 3B

Hit or Miss

Three's A Crowd

Good on Paper

The Abbott Brothers

Rent a Husband

Buy a Boyfriend

Standalones

Don't Mind if "I Do"

About Piper & Rayne

Piper Rayne is a *USA Today* Bestselling Author duo who write "heartwarming humor with a side of sizzle" about families, whether that be blood or found. They both have e-readers full of one-clickable books, they're married to husbands who drive them to drink, and they're both chauffeurs to their kids. Most of all, they love hot heroes and quirky heroines who make them laugh, and they hope you do, too!

www.ingramcontent.com/pod-product-compliance
Lightning Source LLC
Chambersburg PA
CBHW032306310726
48973CB00008B/2543